Murder in the Hoosier Corn

By

Michael H Sibbitt

Edited by

Michael L Sibbitt

Copyright © 2010 by Michael H Sibbitt

2nd Edition, 2012

First published by www.Lulu.com, 2010

All rights reserved. No part of this publication may be reproduced, stored in a retrieval system, or transmitted, in any form or by any means, electronic, mechanical, photocopying, recording, or otherwise, without the prior permission of Michael H Sibbitt.

ISBN: 13 Digit: 978-1463658496
        10 Digit: 1463658494

PREFACE

This novel was inspired by an actual homicide investigation conducted by the author. However, all characters and events in this story are completely fictional, and any similarities to any persons living or dead, and any real or true to life events are purely coincidental.

This story, unfortunately, illustrates man's inhumanity to man—in this particular case, man's inhumanity to woman. It also reflects the failings, frailties, and weaknesses of human beings, and the "human condition." With that being said, it is hoped this story illustrates to the reader a side of life that they seldom, if ever see, especially in scenic southern Indiana.

A word of apology should be made to the more sensitive readers concerning the crude and flagrant language used in much of the dialogue and descriptions in this story. However, in defense of the author, this is exactly how people act, think, and talk in Detective Harry Sullivan's dark world.

It is hoped this story will prove interesting and revealing, and open the reader's eyes to a real life world that actually exists right around them. I hope the reader finds this story revealing, and interesting reading, even if it might not always be enjoyable.

The author would also like to remind the reader of one more thing—please do not associate the exploits, or should I say "sexploits" of the main character, Harry Sullivan, with the author, retired detective Michael H Sibbitt of the Indiana State Police.

A word of thanks should be given to my son for his guidance, and technical assistance in the writing of this short novel. Also, I very much appreciate the encouragement of my wife throughout this writing.

Michael H Sibbitt

FOREWORD

       My dad was gone a lot when I was a kid. Being a police officer will keep a man (or a woman nowadays) away from his family more than it should. At least, that was the way it used to be in the 1970's and 80's. That had a lot to do with why the divorce rate for cops was so high back then. As far as I know, today cops might only work 40 hours a week and have plenty of time for their families. If that is the case, they sure have it better than Dad did.

       I never heard about anything that happened at Dad's job. He was good about keeping all that happened on a daily basis away from me. The only thing I ever heard from him was, "Whatever you do, do not become a police officer!" I guess cases like the one you will read about here affected him in a way that he did not want his only son to experience something similar.

       Later on, once I entered adulthood, Dad told me about some of the cases he worked on. I told him, "You should write a book about that!" He heard that a lot from others as well over the years.

       Personally, I caught the writing bug at 20 years of age. It was then that I began writing a screenplay called *Quick Romances*. It was read by several production companies in Hollywood, but not surprisingly, no one made an offer to buy it. Looking at it fifteen years later, I can see why. It was lousy, even by B-movie standards. Hey, cut me some slack…I was only twenty-one!

       Five years ago, I finished a book called *The Restaurant Jungle*. I made the decision to write it when the technology of self-publishing via the Internet became possible. Now, there was no way you could *not* be a published author as long as you could finish a project. I think once Dad was able to hold and read the finished product authored by his son, the realization came to him that he could accomplish the same goal, which I very much encouraged.

       I am proud of him for starting, but more importantly, completing *Murder in the Hoosier Corn*. Plenty of adults could not even write a simple book report worth reading if they were forced to, much less create a nearly 120 page manuscript. You think it's easy? Just give it a try and see how far you get.

       Good job, Dad.

Michael L Sibbitt
December 2010

The author, as a young Indiana State Police trooper.

TABLE OF CONTENTS

A Gruesome Discovery	Page 8
The Introduction of Beth Cowens	Page 13
Bridgeport's Ingenious Plan	Page 17
The Melinda Mounts Incident	Page 21
The Breakup	Page 25
I Didn't Kill That Little Bitch!	Page 28
A Million Dollar Bond?	Page 34
Are Two Dummies Better Than One?	Page 38
Family Rituals	Page 41
P.E. Teacher, Preacher, or a Cop	Page 44
Informants and Compliments	Page 48
Inquisitions with Scumbags	Page 53
An Overweight Woman Lacking a Few, Sorely-Needed Teeth	Page 60
A Depressed and Worried Man	Page 66
The Trial (Part I)	Page 74
A Barfly and Her Trailer	Page 79
The Trial (Part II)	Page 82
Women Drama	Page 85

The Trial (Part III)	Page 88
The Beauty and the Beast	Page 94
The Trial (Part IV): The Verdict	Page 98
One Last Interview	Page 104
Epilogue	Page 110
In Retrospect	Page 113

CHAPTER ONE - A GRUESOME DISCOVERY

Are you going to eat breakfast or not? I want to get this kitchen cleaned up!
Harry looked in the bathroom mirror to make sure his thinning hair looked satisfactory. If he combed it just right, his receding hairline would magically disappear, along with a few years.
Are you ignoring me?
Harry put his toiletries away and headed towards the annoying voice in the kitchen.
"Did you hear me? Are you having anything for breakfast or are you just having coffee?" Harry's wife demanded to know.
"Just the coffee. Fill me up for the road, will ya?" Harry requested as he handed her his cup.
Harry left without either one of them saying goodbye. This was typical. The bright sun made Harry squint at first. He left his sunglasses in the car the day prior. It was a typical, humid July morning in Southwestern Indiana. Thinking ahead, Harry applied extra deodorant while getting ready. Otherwise, it would have been a long day for anyone unfortunate enough to be in his presence.
Harold 'Harry' Sullivan was having his forth cup of coffee while driving to the Indiana State Police Post. After a few, early-morning bullshit conversations with several coworkers, Sullivan began looking over his stack of manila folders containing the active criminal investigations he was currently working on. Just then, the radio dispatcher buzzed his phone. *It's for you Sullivan. It's the Poland County Sheriff.*
"Harold, this is Roger," the voice on the phone stated. "They've found a body in a cornfield about three miles southwest of Lewisburg off of County Road 1380 West. It looks like it's a young female, left naked and dead out in the cornfield. I've got a couple of deputies standing by at the scene, and they'll protect it until you and your lab people get there."
"Okay, I'm on my way," Sullivan curiously responded.
Grabbing up his folders and quickly exiting the rear of the building, he told the first sergeant on duty what he had, where he was going, and to send the lab people and other key state police personnel that would be needed at the scene. Getting in his unmarked car and heading to the scene, all kinds of emotions already started swirling in his head. After all, a murder like this was certainly not a common thing in the rural parts of Indiana. Sullivan could already feel the self-imposed pressure starting to build, thinking prematurely of

all the things he would want to do once he got to the scene, not to miss anything, and not make any mistakes that might come back to haunt him later. The sweat started to run down his face and soak his shirt, even though it should have been comfortable in his air-conditioned car. It was such a hot, misrible day one could almost cut the humidity with a knife. A person would be challenged to find a place sultrier than Southern Indiana in the middle of summer. Adding to the nearly unbearable weather was a gruesome murder looming on Sullivan's horizon. It was going to be his responsibility to investigate, arrest the perpetrator or perpetrators involved, and successfully solve the case.

When someone thinks of a policeman (especially a detective), the terms confident, qualified, and hands-on might come to mind. Sullivan did not feel that way at all on this particular morning while en route to the scene. Sullivan's mind raced with various thoughts. *Shit, I hope I don't screw anything up or make a bunch of mistakes! This is one I have to solve. The pressure is going to be intense on this one. Who is the girl? What happened to her? Who could have done this in Poland County, Indiana?*

The cornfield was located about a quarter mile off of the county road. The first thing Sullivan observed when he arrived was two deputies, a couple of what appeared to be farmers in overalls, corn stocks that had been flattened in a horseshoe pattern. Upon closer observation, he noticed something lying out in the flattened cornfield about one hundred yards from the lane. At first it appeared to be some kind of animal, perhaps a deer, but upon careful observation it could be seen that it was a human body. It was one of those experiences where you obviously see something, but you momentarily find it hard to believe what you are really seeing. The pressure really starts setting in, like a thick fog that frequently forms in the Indiana countryside.

Upon exiting his commission (cars that are issued to police officers), Sullivan asked the deputies, "Hey. What do we have here?"

"There is a girl…dead, naked, her body out there in the corn field. The owner of the farm ground found her just after daybreak, when he came out to check his crops. I went out and took a look at her, and then roped the scene off so no one would disturb it. Oh, by the way," the deputy matter-of-factly mentioned, "her face is gone."

Sullivan had just exited his vehicle, when his best friend, confidant, and Indiana State Police lab tech Joe Rallings arrived. Rallings was one of the most talented guys on the department. He was the type of guy that someone would want with them if they were a soldier in a foxhole. He was not only very good at everything he did, he was a straight shooter and honest to a fault. Obviously, Sullivan was relieved and happy when he saw Rallings pull up. At least he wouldn't be alone on this.

An Indiana State Police detective was a rather unique police officer for several reasons. He was considered the professional, especially in the smaller communities and rural parts of the state. He investigated all serious crimes and did not specialize. The felonies included in this list were murder, robberies, forgeries, thefts, rapes, and every other serious crime that was on the books. Also, when he investigated something extremely serious, like a homicide, he worked it from start to finish. He did not concern himself about overtime or going home after his shift was up. In fact, the Indiana State Police did not have such a thing as overtime in those days, the 1960's and 1970's.

As soon as Sullivan got the initial call, and especially after he arrived on the scene and saw the corpse in the cornfield, he knew this was going to be a long, rough, pressure-packed investigation; so he may as well prepare for the long haul. After interviewing the owner of the ground, who initially discovered the body, Sullivan ordered everyone to leave the scene except for police personnel and the county coroner. As a matter of fact, he posted an officer at the starting point of the dirt lane that led back to the cornfield from the gravel county road. The officer was told to let no one but authorized personnel back to the scene.

Just then, Sullivan and Rallings noticed tire tracks in the sandy soil. Close by were shoe prints, all of which were carefully measured and photographed. Next, they approached the body, carefully walking over the knocked-down corn stocks. Rallings was taking numerous photographs as they approached the corpse. The female lying on her side appeared to be young, in her late teens or twenties. She was nude, with developed breasts, reddish-brown hair, and a matured pubic area. A closer observation indicated what appeared to be bullet holes in her back. Next to those were cuts, appearing as though they were carefully and purposely carved into her torso. Her face was unrecognizable, looking like a mass of blood and flesh with no features one could distinguish in order to visually reveal the identity of the young woman. A quick visual examination of the vaginal area indicated that the young woman had sex recently, as the vaginal lips were gaping open.

Before long, Sullivan noticed a chrome strip, possibly from a vehicle of some kind, located among the corn stocks that were laying flat against the soil. Once the strip was photographed, it was carefully picked up, in order to not disturb any evidence that might be on it such as fingerprints, and placed in the back of Sullivan's unmarked police car. Sullivan and Rallings spent the entire day carefully processing the scene before the body was removed and transported to the local funeral home. The body was accompanied by the coroner to establish a tight chain of custody reference any evidence that might later be obtained from the body.

Before Sullivan went to the funeral home, he made a quick detour. On a hunch, he went to a body shop owned by an individual whom he knew, who had repaired wrecked vehicles for years. It was past quitting time, but the body man was still there working on a vehicle when Sullivan pulled up.

"Hey Joe," Sullivan said, "I want you to take a look at something for me."

Sullivan pulled the chrome strip out from the backseat of his car and asked Joe if he had any idea what type of vehicle this chrome strip may have originated from.

Joe carefully examined it and responded, "Yeah, I would say that came off of a Ford Ranchero or Chevrolet El Camino; lime green in color since there are flakes of paint on it where it was masked off for painting." Sullivan put this information into his mental rolodex.

Upon arrival at the funeral home, Rallings and the coroner were already there waiting for him. The body was still covered in the same white sheet that had been wrapped around it at the scene. This was to retain any evidence that might be on the body so it wouldn't be lost in the transport. The girl, whoever she was, had several silver and turquoise rings on her fingers, which was a style of jewelry that was popular at that particular time. The sight of this poor, unfortunate girl, with her face obliterated and her torso, front and back, covered in bullet holes, lacerations, bruises, blood, and dirt, would have been enough to make the average person vomit. However, that was one thing that policemen and soldiers seem to have in common—somehow learning how to cope with something that the normal person could not, without going totally nuts or blowing their own brains out.

Sullivan carefully examined the body, especially her face (what was left of it), trying to determine if the deceased was someone he had dealings with prior. He tried to imagine what she went through before dying and who the cruel, brutal, sick son-of-a bitches were who could do this kind of thing to a young woman.

Rallings interrupted Sullivan's thoughts by telling him that he needed to get the body to Morganville in order for an autopsy to be conducted by the only forensic pathologist in the tri-state area. Sullivan responded before he did that, he wanted to make a few inquiries with the local police and see if they had any information on any runaways or any local girls they thought this could possibly be. He wanted to find someone who might be a relative, friend or acquaintance of the deceased to come to the funeral home to see if they could identify her.

That inquiry seemed to be worthless at first. However, Sullivan did get one name of a local girl that was rumored to be pretty wild and fit the general description of the victim. Sullivan knew the uncle of the girl in question, because he was a local school administrator named Bill Furrows. Sullivan had dealings with him in the past in his capacity as a state police officer. Sullivan telephoned Furrows, explained the situation to him, and asked if he could come to the funeral home to try to identify the girl as being his niece. He reluctantly agreed, and drove up to the funeral home. Sullivan warned him that it was a gruesome sight, trying to prepare him for what he was about to see. The sheet was pulled back, and the uncle carefully looked at the body. It seemed like forever, with his face turning almost as white as the sheet the girl was wrapped in. Bill Furrows asked to step out of the room and Sullivan followed him.

"I don't know if that's my niece or not. Hell, her face is gone!" Furrows exclaimed.

After stating the obvious and being of little help, Furrows left. Sullivan then told Rallings to go ahead and accompany the corpse to Morganville for the autopsy.

Sullivan drove home in a haze. He was mentally exhausted but slept little. Thoughts of the case ran through his mind all night as he tossed and turned.

"Stop moving so much. You're keeping me up," Sullivan's wife complained.

She had the luxury of not seeing what Sullivan just did earlier in the day. If she did, she wouldn't be sleeping much either.

CHAPTER TWO - THE INTRODUCTION OF BETH COWENS

Beth Cowens was not your normal looking fourteen year-old girl. She did have an innocent-enough looking, cute face. On that fourteen year-old face were big blue eyes, reddish brown hair, and a pointed little nose. However, any similarities to an innocent teenager in physical attributes, lifestyle, and conduct, ended there. Generally speaking, Beth was curvaceous, similar to a well-built, grown woman. Her shapely long legs topped off her feminine appeal as a sensual female, rather than a typical fourteen year-old girl.

It was another sticky Southern Indiana evening, and Beth was getting ready to go out to party. She was dressed in a tank top with no bra, tight blue jean shorts, and a pair of flip-flop shoes showing off her painted, red toenails. Plenty of inexpensive jewelry adorned parts of her body. Yes, it was fair to say she was dressed to party hard, early-eighties style.

She told her little sister she was going out, and slammed the screen door as she exited. Beth started her usual walking tour down Main Street of Glen Burnie, which was a metropolis of about 7500 souls in the heart of Hoosierland. She was hoping to meet up with some friends, or even better, the older guy she had been seeing recently. 'Seeing' was a nice term to describe her dealings with her man. In reality, she had been having sex, drinking, and using drugs with him. Several vehicles whizzed by. The drivers and passengers yelled at Beth.

How 'bout a piece of ass?"

"Come on! Let's party, baby!"

Beth had been walking up and down Main Street for an hour or so, when her 'main squeeze' slowly drove by in his old, rusted-out truck. She yelled at him to pull over at the local car wash. Beth got inside.

"Hey, what's going on tonight?" Beth asked.

"I've got a fifth of Jack Daniels. I should be able to score some pot too," he answered.

He then put his vehicle in gear, and headed north on Main Street. Beth's boyfriend was a local low-life named Larry Bridgeport. He was twenty-five years old, and was well-known by the local police, mainly for using and selling drugs. He had also been arrested for theft, burglary, and a variety of misdemeanors. This included DUI, reckless driving, and assault and battery. However, that did not deter Beth. To her, that made him even *more* exciting. After all, he was a bad boy, and that was not a character flaw in her young, immature eyes. It was an asset.

Beth came from a family that were thought to be poor white trash to most of the so-called upstanding citizens of Glen Burnie. She had several brothers and sisters, totaling seven including herself, with an older sister and brother already deceased. The sister died from an accident as a passenger on a motorcycle, and the brother from an overdose. Beth did attend school. However, academics were not her priority. She made poor grades, was frequently was absent from school, and had already been suspended several times from middle school for violations of school rules, regulations, and policies.

As Beth and Bridgeport cruised around town, she turned up the bottle of Jack Daniels and took a big swig. She coughed and choked on the foul-tasting whiskey, almost to the point of vomiting. To act more grown-up than she really was she declared how great it tasted and that she was ready to get high. Bridgeport took a big drink of the whiskey himself as he headed out of town to a destination where he thought he could get what they needed to have his type of good time.

After driving about ten minutes on one of the local gravel roads, he pulled up into a yard where several other vehicles were parked. A single light was on outside over the door of a rather shabby, beaten up, mobile home.

"We're here. Let's go inside," exclaimed Bridgeport before tongue-kissing Beth.

As they exited the truck and approached the trailer, the sound of hard rock music could be heard, indicating that they had indeed located the scene they were looking for. Now, it was time to have some fun. In Bridgeport's mind, this meant drinking, using drugs, and having sex. Bridgeport knocked on the door.

"Yeah, who is it?" the person behind the door asked.

"It's Tater. Open up!"

The door swung open. Tater and Beth entered into a sea of cigarette, marijuana, and hashish smoke that was so thick it nearly burned their eyes as they entered the dingy trailer. There appeared to be fifteen to twenty young, hippie-looking men and women sprawled around everywhere. The hard rock music coming from the stereo was so loud, the sound was almost distorted. Every person in the trailer appeared extremely intoxicated from one substance or another. Most were in various stages of being undressed, with a couple of them totally naked. The others still had a few bits of clothing on. Yes, there was little doubt that Tater felt at home in this type of environment.

The person who owned the trailer and the little patch of ground in this isolated, rural area, was a black guy known to be a local drug dealer named Joe Black. His nickname was "Tricky," and unknown to the other local dopers, he was a police informant when it was to his advantage. Others in attendance were the local drug users and other various forms of human debris of Poland County.

There were several of Tater's friends and acquaintances in attendance, such as Harry Seasons, who had a pock-marked face and was a sex pervert. Cliff Queen and Kevin Bigley, who were both low-life dopers who, many would say, were not worth the powder and lead to blow them up. There were numerous, other similar types there. A person would be hard pressed to find aspiring doctors, lawyers or engineers present. After an hour of hard partying, Tater Bridgeport asked the host, Tricky, if he had any coke.

Tricky responded in the affirmative with the sophisticated response of "Fuck yeah, man."

Not wanting to share with everyone in the living room, Tricky and Tater graduated to a tiny bedroom in the trailer and closed the door. Tater whipped out a few lines of low-quality coke, which had been cut so many times before it reached its final destination, probably contained more baking soda than cocaine. Tater proceeded over to a spot on the floor in front of a glass-top cocktail table. Wanting some female company, he yelled for Beth. One of the partygoers opened the door to inform Tater that she was passed out in the bathroom and had thrown up all over the floor around the toilet.

Stupid fuckin' bitch, Tater thought to himself.

There went his plan to get laid tonight. Tater then proceeded to chop out a line on the glass table, pulled out a straw, and made the cocaine disappear. The party lasted until daylight, with most everyone passed out. A night of sex, drugs, and rock-and-roll was the norm for young, restless people in boring Poland County, Indiana.

Around noon, Beth woke up lying on the old couch that was on the front porch of her house. It was not made for outdoor use. In her Podunk town though, it was considered fine, outdoor furniture. She remembered little about the previous night, and didn't know how she got home or who brought her there. She assumed it must have been Bridgeport. All she knew was that she felt and smelled horrible. Mosquito bites were all over her legs and itched like crazy.

Just then, the screen door slammed open. Her mother burst out of the door, screaming at her. She told Beth she was going to get knocked up, put in jail, or killed if she didn't change her lifestyle. Her mother pleaded with Beth to stop staying out all night and hanging with the crowd she heard awful rumors about. Beth did not say anything. She simply went in the house to take a bath and put something on the bites to keep them from itching. Her mother just shook her head in frustration while lighting a cigarette.

Beth woke up around 6pm, and went through the same procedure, getting ready to go out again. She walked down south Main Street when she ran into a couple of her girlfriends, Melinda Mounts and Jill Rock. She asked them if they had seen Bridgeport.

"No. Haven't you heard? He got picked up early this morning for drunk driving," Jill responded.

Beth surmised that must have happened after he had dropped her off at her house. It did not bother her too terribly much. She was just glad she was not with him when he got stopped by the police. She figured that somebody else would pick her up and she would simply party with them instead. After all, she knew she was good looking, built the way older guys liked, and was willing to give them what they wanted. She had not walked very long when a black Ford pulled into the car wash parking lot. The driver asked her to come over. She did and noticed it was a boy she knew who was two or three years older than her named Dusty Harrison.

After a couple of minutes of preliminary conversation, Beth got in his car and he headed straight to the country. He had a case of beer iced down in the back seat and told Beth to get them a couple out of the cooler. He turned the radio up to a volume level that caused the cheap, factory speakers in the back window to vibrate. Yes, it was party time again. Harrison drove along the county roads for about fifteen or twenty minutes until he pulled next to an old stripper pit. They talked for about an hour about the big shindig the previous night, Bridgeport getting picked up by the police, and various other subjects like, who was screwing who.

When Dusty thought Beth had enough beer in her, he reached over and gave her a sloppy, wet kiss, sticking his tongue about as far down her throat as was possible. She responded by doing the same thing. He then reached under her blouse and massaged her large breasts, getting them unharnessed. Although Beth was only fourteen, she was not shy. She reached down and unzipped his jeans and pulled his penis out, which was about as hard and rigid as a tire tool. With his help, she took her own shorts and underwear off, and laid down in the front seat of the car, waiting for Dusty to maneuver between her legs. He finally managed to do that, but was having some sort of problem making insertion, apparently due to the cramped quarters of the front seat. Beth thought she would help and reached down to grab the business end of Dusty, deciding to take care of the insertion procedure herself. In no time at all, she heard Dusty moan to which she realized he had just crash-landed prior to even taking off. Not surprisingly, there wasn't much conversation between the two on the ride home.

CHAPTER THREE - BRIDGEPORT'S INGENIOUS PLAN

      The next day was little different than all other days during this long hot summer. However, Beth did not wake up on the front porch couch on this occasion. Around 2pm, she woke up in her own bed, in her extremely messy room. Her crotch area felt completely violated. Her mouth felt like an army had marched through it. She had a horrible headache to boot. She thought about taking a bath but decided against it since she was heading over to the public swimming pool. After all, floating in the pool water for a few hours and allowing the chlorine do it's sanitizing should do the trick for her to be ready for the evening's activities. All she had to do was dress, brush her hair, put on an excessive amount of makeup, and spray on some cheap perfume. After returning home from the swimming pool, the phone rang. It was the newfound love of her life, Tater Bridgeport. He told her he would be by about 7pm to pick her up. Making things interesting to Beth, Tater mentioned that he had something to talk to her about.

      After picking her up, he informed her that he had a proposition for her where they both could make some money. He told Beth he found a good contact to buy all of the marijuana and hash he could sell. He thought about using Beth and some of her girlfriends to form a prostitution ring, which would open up an outlet to sell his weed and possibly some cocaine, if he could get his hands on some. He told her, being juveniles, she and her girlfriends could not get in any serious trouble; not to mention, they could make good money. He continued, stating that Beth would be the only one who would know about him as the originator of this scheme and supplier of the dope. That way, no one could rat on him since they would not have direct knowledge of his involvement or the level of it. Bridgeport told Beth that if she loved him, she would do this.

      "Hey babe, you can make some easy money for us and your friends. Hell, you probably won't even have to screw anybody; just blow jobs and hand jobs will be enough," Tater informed her.

      Unfortunately, Beth had little guidance in her life regarding right and wrong, which of course, was no fault of her own. Adding to that, she did not want to disappoint the man she thought she was madly in love with. Beth was simply a kid looking for love and attention. Consequently, she stated that she would check with some of her girlfriends to see if they might be interested in his proposition. Bridgeport mentioned that he thought of this idea while talking to some fellow inmates at the county jail a couple of nights prior. He did not mention to her that he needed money to pay support on a kid and for a lawyer resulting from his latest run-in with the law. What he did tell her was that he and Beth could run off, get married, and live happily ever after. Like most dopers and criminals, getting a legitimate job to pay their bills and expenses in life was nearly out of the question. Beth, being a gullible, young girl, believed everything Bridgeport said, regardless of how outlandish or improbable it was.

A few days later, Beth met with some girlfriends and acquaintances of hers who were all under eighteen to explain "her" idea of how to make some easy money. Unfortunately, they were cut from the same cloth as Beth, and her ideas did not shock or turn them off in any way. She told them that they could not really get in any big trouble because they were all juveniles. If they were ever questioned by the police they should simply say nothing. In fact, the police could not even question them without their parent or guardian's presence and consent (Bridgeport, being the jailhouse lawyer he was, educated her on this fact). After a few questions from the girls, they all agreed it was a good plan to make easy money. One girl even said it sounded like fun.

A couple of weeks went by with little new or exciting happening. One evening, Bridgeport called Beth and told her to meet him by the car wash on South Main Street. Tater informed Beth that a couple of older guys he knew wanted a "piece of ass." Sweetening the deal, Tater mentioned that they would probably buy some dope as well. He told the guys he knew where they could "get a little," but they could only get a hand job for twenty dollars. If they wanted a blow job, that would be thirty dollars. If they had the desire to go all out and have regular sex, that would cost fifty dollars. They told Bridgeport they would pay twenty dollars apiece for blow jobs, assuming it was a good-looking girl. Bridgeport made the deal, and had already collected the money from the guys.

"All you have to do is take care of business," Tater informed Beth.

Although she had agreed to this arrangement, she was a little confused and thought for a brief moment that it was strange if Bridgeport loved her like he said he did, he would be okay with her giving two strangers blowjobs. However, that thought passed swiftly, and she proceeded over to the black Trans-Am that was parked by the car wash with two guys sitting in it. Bridgeport told her he would give her twenty dollars (her cut) when she got back.

Beth got into the backseat of the Trans-Am. She was surprised at first because they looked like they were in their thirties, which was a little older than what she was expecting. They were both smoking weed and asked her if she wanted a hit. Beth put the marijuana joint in her mouth and inhaled deeply. The first drag burned her throat and lungs, causing her to cough loudly; but that did not deter her from taking another drag. In her mind, this was going to make the job more tolerable. The guy in the passenger seat gave her an unopened bottle of Old Crow whiskey, and suggested she take a drink.

After about ten minutes, the driver pulled in to a lane that seemed to go nowhere and parked.

"I'm first," the driver said.

He got in the backseat where Beth was sitting. He began sloppily kissing her, and shoved his filthy hand up her short, blue jeans skirt, pulling her underwear to the side. He then rudely shoved half of his hand up her vagina.

She screamed at the top of her lungs, "Hey! That hurts!"

"You're paid for! Do what you're told!" he reminded her.

It was too uncomfortable in the back seat so he proceeded to drag her out of the car and lean her over the trunk of the car. He pulled up her skirt, tore her panties completely off, and threw them on the ground. The next thing Beth knew, the other guy pinned her arms over the trunk while the driver was inside of her, humping like a jackhammer. Thankfully for Beth, after about a dozen thrusts, the driver finished and pulled out.

He then walked around and held Beth's arms while the second guy stuck his unusually large member in her. She screamed in pain, but that did not deter the guy from shoving his penis in and out of her like a piston pumping on a well-tuned V-8 motor. Once he finished, both guys got in the black Trans-Am and sped away, raising dust and gravel in their wake.

"You bastards!" Beth screamed, mostly to herself since no one was there to listen.

Beth did not know where she was at or how to get back to town. She started walking down the gravel road, with only the light of the moon to guide her on an otherwise pitch-black night. She walked for what seemed like for days when she saw the dim lights of Glen Burnie in the distance. She was mad, crying, and generally pissed off; not so much for what these two monsters did to her, but the fact that she had to walk all the way back to town in the pitch dark with Bridgeport nowhere in sight. Even with her inexperience and gullibility, she was beginning to think maybe Bridgeport did not really love her after all and was not as concerned about her welfare as he claimed he was.

As she walked into town up South Main Street, she saw Bridgeport drive by. She yelled at him in order to get his attention, to which he pulled over.

She ran up to his vehicle and started screaming, "Do you know what those two no-good motherfuckers did to me?"

She proceeded to tell the entire story of the evening's unpleasant activities. Bridgeport, being the con man he was, pretended to sympathize with her; telling her he would kill them if and when he ever saw them again. Of course, he also mentioned that this sort-of-thing would never happen again. He tried to console and convince her that this was just an isolated incident. He begrudgingly gave her twenty dollars and drove her home. Once they arrived, Bridgeport gave her a good night kiss like they were young lovers on a first innocent date. He drove away unhappy that he had to give Beth the $20 to keep her halfway satisfied and in line.

CHAPTER FOUR - THE MELINDA MOUNTS INCIDENT

Things were going pretty well for Bridgeport in his newfound business of selling drugs and sex. The girls were getting rid of just about all of the dope supplied to them, so there was not much concern about that part of the business. Since this was Bridgeport's first venture into this kind of enterprise, he figured the sex part was just operating expenses that were a bonus to the customer in order to sell him more dope. However, a couple of incidents early on threatened to derail his business before he really got it going.

Melinda Mounts made a deal with a couple of locals to provide them with a hundred dollars worth of cocaine. She met them on the town square in Glen Burnie. They insisted she accompany them to a remote area where they would snort some of the blow to make sure it was decent quality. She agreed, especially since that seemed like a bonus to her—get high and make some easy money.

Melinda squeezed between the driver and the passenger, headed for a night of excitement. They drove about twenty minutes until they were in a very rural area in Carroll County. They parked behind a big sycamore tree to hide their vehicle so they would not be disturbed. Local deputy sheriffs and state troopers made it a habit of driving around, looking for underage kids drinking.

The driver, who stated that his name was Jack, turned the volume on the stereo up, way past the point of what the factory speakers could stand. Everyone got out of the vehicle. Jack grabbed a fifth of Jack Daniels and passed it around in order to get everyone in the mood. The cocaine was then spread across the hood of his Corvette, and each one proceeded to snort it until there was nothing left. For some men, cocaine provided a high that was similar to modern day Viagra—a hard-on that lasted all night. In this particular instance, that seemed to be the case.

Jack and the other guy, allegedly named Bono, decided that it was time to take advantage of the situation at hand. Their intention was to screw every orifice in Melinda's body. Unbeknownst to them, Melinda was sick to her stomach due to the whiskey and cocaine that she had ingested. Vomit flew everywhere. Sex, drugs, and rock n' roll was the furthest thing from her mind. That did not bother Jack or Bono though. Their evening of debauchery had just begun. Bono grabbed Melinda and started pulling at her shirt.

"Why don't you come over here? I want you to suck me off."

He pulled his member out and started forcing her head down, while Melinda protested and pleaded the entire time. Bono lost his temper and pushed her to the ground, startling her. Then, he began hitting her in the face with his closed fists and screaming at her.

"You little prick teaser! Do what you're told!"

Frightened to death, Melinda suddenly became quiet and failed to move. Bono realized his plans had gone awry so he simply jacked off and ejaculated on Melinda's face.

He then told Jack, "Hey, you'd better get some of this while you can. I shut the little bitch up!"

Jack then proceeded to pull off her blue jeans shorts and underwear and got between her legs. Melinda did not move or make a sound the entire time. After he finished, Jack stood over her like a hunter admiring the trophy deer that he killed.

Just when Jack was feeling triumphant, the drugs and alcohol began taking its toll. He suddenly felt sick and began vomiting all over the young girl lying at his feet. Then, for good measure, Bono kicked Melinda a couple of times in the ribs, while Melinda let out a weeping cry.

Bono laughed and told Jack, "Hell, I guess she's still alive. Fuck it. Let's get out of here."

Jack and Bono got in the Corvette and took off in a cloud of dirt and gravel dust, leaving the young girl behind lying on the ground. They were kind enough to leave her with a tooth knocked out and a black eye.

Melinda opened her eyes only to realize she was in a hospital bed, in the Poland County Memorial Hospital. Her face and head were wrapped up like a mummy. She had small holes in the bandages in order to see, but could not see anything but foggy brightness due to the swelling. She panicked at first, not remembering anything about the previous night. The pain was intolerable. She began screaming; wanting someone to recognize her existence, inform her of where she was at, and to remind her of what had happened. A nurse finally came to her aid and told her she was going to be okay. Melinda drifted off again into unconsciousness, and unbeknown to her, did not wake up again until the next day.

Melinda finally woke up, still confused and in pain. The day she was out of it gave her a chance to physically recover from the beating she had received. A nurse working in intensive care realized she was awake and proceeded to comfort her by telling her she was going to be alright. Melinda began asking the nurse an array of questions.

"What happened to me?"

"How did I get here?"

"Where is my mom?"

The nurse responded she did not know the answers to any of those questions, but the doctor would be around to see her when he made his rounds.

About thirty minutes later, the doctor did make his rounds, and proceeded to try to answer some of her questions about her physical condition. He told her she was lucky to be alive; and nonchalantly listed her injuries as a broken nose, a couple of crushed bones in her face, a missing tooth, and a concussion. He also informed her she would need some surgery to repair the damage that had been done to her face, but she could expect to make a full recovery. With that, the doctor said he would return on the next morning's rounds, and in the meantime she would be moved out of intensive care to a regular hospital room. Melinda started to ask the doctor some more questions, but he told her he was on a tight schedule and left.

After being moved to a regular room, the bandages were mostly removed from her swollen and disfigured face. On the bright side, she could see and hear clearly. She had numerous tubes inserted in her, including one that carried nourishment to her body since she could not eat due to her mouth being so swollen and sore. She had various other wires attached to her, which were connected to various monitors around the room.

Melinda looked up to see a big guy, in his late thirties, wearing a suit, standing next to her bed looking down at her. He was not an ugly man per say, but someone certainly would not mistake him for John Travolta. He did have the appearance of being a mean, no-nonsense looking type of guy; someone Melinda immediately thought she did not want to mess with. She did not recognize him, but right away she instinctively knew he was probably a police officer of some sort. He looked like a poster child for a cop, with his short hair, serious look, and a mustache that curled around the corners of his mouth. If he was not an officer of the law, he looked like one of those hitmen for the mafia that were frequently on television shows.

"Melinda, my name is Harry Sullivan. I'm a state police detective, and I'm here to check on what happened to you and who did it," Sullivan informed her.

At first, Melinda didn't know what to say. Then she remembered what Beth told her about talking to the police…don't do it! After a minute of stalling, she finally responded to the detective.

"I'm not sure. I don't remember anything. The last thing I remember is walking down Main Street."

Melinda felt the police probably could not catch the guys anyway since she did not know who they were or what their names were. Making an arrest even more remote, she did not recall what they looked like or what occurred during the evening in question. She thought by talking to the police they would for sure get into her activities, what she had been doing, and whom she was associated with. Melinda was smart enough to know she wanted to avoid that at all costs. In order to end the conversation, she asked for the nurse, indicating that she was in excruciating pain and could not remember anything so it was useless to talk any further. Detective Sullivan, not believing a word she said concerning her denial of remembering anything about the assault, left frustrated. Did she not realize he was there to help her?

Sullivan had not been gone thirty minutes when Beth Cowens appeared at Melinda's hospital room. Bridgeport brought her to the hospital. This was not to check on her condition, but more like to find out what happened and if the police got to her yet. He did not go into the hospital room, but instead stayed out in the lounge. He instructed Beth to find out everything she could and not mention his name. Beth was to tell Melinda that a "friend" brought her to the hospital, and to leave it at that.

Beth, at first was shocked at her friend's appearance. She walked over and hugged her.

"What happened? Who did this to you?"

Melinda proceeded to tell her the entire story; what she remembered anyway. She also informed her that a state police detective had already been to the hospital, but she did not tell him anything. One thing was for sure. Melinda was no scholar; but after her recent experience that put her in the hospital, she was definitely out of the drug and sex trade.

CHAPTER FIVE - THE BREAKUP

The Melinda Mounts incident definitely threw a monkey wrench into Bridgeport's business plan. When the other girls found out about what happened to Melinda, they flew the coup like a homing pigeon on the fly. They confided to Beth that they were afraid what happened to Melinda would happen to them. They wanted no part of that kind of party. Beth informed Bridgeport of the news, which infuriated him. He blamed Beth and instructed her to try to convince the girls this was an isolated incident and would not happen again. Beth said she would try, but she knew the probability of the girls changing their minds was doubtful, due to the fact they were all scared to death. However, due to her undying devotion to Bridgeport, Beth was going to try to get the girls to reconsider. If that did not work, she would attempt recruiting new girls. Bridgeport had her convinced that nothing bad would happen again.

The conversation involving the girls never took place due to another incident that occurred shortly after the one involving Melinda. This really put an end to the business venture once and for all. News of the newfound availability of drugs in the area got around and the police, of course, got wind of it. One of the girls, Jill Rock, told Beth she would continue selling as a favor to her and see how it went. A couple of weeks after the Melinda Mounts incident, Jill was advised there was a guy inquiring where he could buy a large amount of hashish and marijuana. Jill made arrangements to meet with the guy and try to make a deal with him.

Jill met with the guy in the parking lot of a local tavern called the Big Track Lounge. Jill got in his car, which was parked in the corner of the parking lot. She got into an older, beat-up Ford, faded red in color. Behind the wheel sat a big guy, in his thirties, with long hair and a beard. He told Jill his name was Mike and he was from Morganville. He continued, stating he wanted to purchase some hash and marijuana, and had about five hundred dollars to spend. She made arrangements to meet him the next night at the same time and the same location. Jill was not very sophisticated in this business, and never gave a thought that this might be a setup.

The next night she showed up with the hash and marijuana wrapped up in grocery sacks. She got in the vehicle and gave the grocery sacks to Mike. He checked out the dope to make sure it was legitimate. After this was taken care of, he gave Beth five $100 bills, which the police had already marked for identification purposes. Jill got out of the car and started walking, while the beat-up Ford sped away. She had not gotten a block up the road when a marked state police car pulled up beside of her. Two uniformed troopers calmly walked over to Jill and informed her she was under arrest for the sale of narcotics. They handcuffed her, put her in the back of the police car, and proceeded to the Poland County Jail.

Once they got up to the sheriff's office, Jill's parents were contacted. Jill remembered what Beth told her about not saying anything to the police. After her parents arrived, they were told what she had been arrested for. They were given a few minutes to confer with Jill alone. She was then advised of her rights before questioning commenced. Jill claimed no knowledge of the entire incident, and concluded that it must have been some sort of mistaken identity. The officer in charge asked her to explain the $500 in her purse. She stammered, saying it was money from a friend that was owed to her. The officer then took the five one hundred dollar bills and showed them to Jill. He pointed out the markings on them, proving that they were the two bills paid to her by the drug dealer. Jill continued to deny knowing what the officer was talking about, claiming no knowledge of the drug deal. She kept saying over and over in her head to not tell the police anything, just as Beth had instructed her to do. Her mother made the comment maybe they should consult with an attorney, which ended any further questioning. The officers informed Jill and her parents that this was a very serious offense. If their daughter continued to be uncooperative, they would attempt to get Jill tried as an adult. It did not help Jill's case considering that she was only a month away from turning eighteen. The police thought this information (threat) might convince her to rat on anyone else involved, especially the person or persons who supplied her with the drugs.

Sullivan was frustrated regarding the battered girl in the hospital not telling him anything, especially since he knew she was lying through her teeth. He could not understand the mentality of kids today. All he was trying to do was help her and arrest the bastards who did this to her. One would think a rural county in Southern Indiana would not have the kind of problems it had been experiencing with crime and immorality. But ever since the upheaval of the 1960's concerning drugs, sex, and the revolt and disrespect against authority, things had pretty much turned to shit. People like Detective Sullivan were left to deal with the end result.

Of course, he heard rumors about all of the drugs that had been going through Poland County lately. He figured it was probably the same menaces to society that he had been dealing with for years. On the top of his list of people supplying drugs was Tater Bridgeport. Sullivan had known the Bridgeport name for almost the entire time he had been a trooper and a detective in Poland County. Tater's father, Andy, owned a tavern in Glen Burnie. In addition to that business, he was also rumored to buy and sell stolen property, deal drugs, and basically do anything and everything known to man in order to make an illegal buck. His tavern, called the Longhorn Saloon, was also known for its bookmaking activities. It also employed strippers, called go-go dancers at that time. They provided extracurricular activities for the lowlife patrons that frequented the place. To have an establishment like that in a small town like Glen Burnie was unusual. For some reason, however, the prosecutor, local police, and general public seemed to tolerate it. Glen Burnie was known for its illegal gambling, and other accompanying activities, which seemed to flourish. The old saying, "the apple does not fall far from the tree," was certainly true concerning the activities, lifestyle, and attitudes of Tater Bridgeport and his father.

Bridgeport lost his salesgirls after the incidents of the beating of Melinda Mounts and the arrest of Jill Rock. After the arrest, Beth no longer attempted to convince the girls to continue on with Bridgeport's scheme. A rape and an arrest were a little too much for these fourteen and fifteen year-old girls. Bridgeport and Beth continued to sell the drugs regardless. Unknown to Beth, Bridgeport was selling drugs provided by someone else, namely his father. On one particular evening, Beth and Bridgeport got into a confrontation over a few topics. One regarded him not giving her the money they had agreed on when they started. The other was her finding out about his philandering ways.

"You son-of-a-bitch! Not only are you not paying me for the shit I've been selling, but you've also been screwing other girls! I thought you loved me. I ought to just turn you in to the fuckin' cops."

That immediately infuriated Bridgeport. Without warning, he whacked Beth in the face, causing the blood and snot to fly. She fell to the ground and began crying.

"You little bitch! If you tell the pigs anything I'll fuckin' kill you!" Bridgeport warned her.

With that, Beth slowly picked herself up off the ground and began running up Main Street toward home thinking, *You fucking asshole, I'll get you back if it's the last thing I do.*

Little did she know then how true these words would turn out to be.

CHAPTER SIX - I DIDN'T KILL THAT LITTLE BITCH!

Accompanied by lab tech Joe Rallings, the body of the deceased was transported from the funeral home to Morganville for the autopsy. Sullivan had all kinds of thoughts racing through his head. One of those told him to head toward South Main Street and check vehicles. He was looking for a lime green El Camino or Ranchero with a chrome strip missing. Sullivan knew the chances of locating a vehicle of that description were about as likely as him making love to his fantasy woman, Dolly Parton, but he had to try anyway. He decided to go to a particular area of town because the Big Track Lounge and its lowlife patrons were located in this rundown neighborhood.

Sullivan ran by the sheriff's office to pick up a friend of his, Deputy George Barney, to accompany him. Sullivan figured he could throw scenarios Barney's way and see what he thought about the investigation. Sullivan proceeded down South Main Street and pulled his vehicle in the parking lot separating the Big Track Lounge and Sal's Liquor Store. There, he began observing traffic as vehicles slowly cruised by. He and Barney were discussing the homicide in reference to who the unidentified victim could be and who could have done something like this. Sullivan and Barney had not been there more than five minutes when a white-over-lime green Chevrolet El Camino drove by, moving at a slow rate of speed.

"Did you see what I just saw? I can't believe it. We haven't been here five minutes!" Sullivan exclaimed.

Sullivan no more than got the words out of his mouth regarding the El Camino, when the car pulled into the parking lot of Sal's Liquor Store. A dirty-looking, white male in his mid-twenties, wearing blue jeans with no shirt or shoes, got out of the vehicle and went into the liquor store. Sullivan parked his car directly behind the truck so he could not escape. Sullivan and Barney got out of their vehicle, and started inspecting it.

Still in a stage of disbelief, Sullivan observed corn stalks sticking out between the doors and the undercarriage. In addition to those, there were numerous .22 caliber shell casings in the bed of the truck. Adding to the evidence list, Sullivan viewed a necklace lying in the front seat, as if it had been torn off of someone's neck.

"Can you believe this? Look at this, George…the corn stocks, the shell casings, the necklace. What do you think?"

Before George could comment, the young male exited the liquor store, carrying a six-pack of beer. He looked at Sullivan with a deer-in-the-headlights-look.

"What do you want with me, Sullivan? I didn't kill that little bitch!" he stammered.

Sullivan immediately grabbed him by the shoulders and shoved him hard up against the El Camino. That was quickly followed by handcuffs and the notice that he was under arrest for murder. Even though he really did not want to advise him of his constitutional rights after witnessing what was left of the victim, he did so anyway because that was his duty. Sullivan made sure to make a mental note of Bridgeport's comment about killing the girl. How could Bridgeport have known anyone had been killed or a body had been found unless Bridgeport had been there?

Sullivan asked Barney to drive Bridgeport's vehicle to the jail so it could be processed by the lab techs. He took a protesting Tater Bridgeport to jail so he could be processed, questioned, and incarcerated.

"I don't know why you motherfuckin' pigs are always hassling me! Man, I haven't done nothin' but mind my own business!" Bridgeport argued.

After arriving at the sheriff's office, Sullivan mugged and printed Bridgeport. Then, he took him in to the small interrogation room, and for good measure, advised him of his rights again. Sullivan gave him the opportunity to sign the "Advice of Rights Interrogation" waiver form. For whatever reason, Bridgeport suddenly got corporative, and signed the form.

"Fuck yeah, I'll sign it and talk to you. I ain't got nothin' to hide."

Sullivan retrieved his tape recorder to record the interrogation. After some preliminary questions such as full name, date of birth, etc., Sullivan began the questioning in earnest. He asked Bridgeport about the comment he made in reference to "not killing that little bitch," when he exited the liquor store. Sullivan wondered how Bridgeport could have even known about a body being found.

"Hell, man. It's been all over town that a girl was found murdered in a cornfield. I've had two or three people mention it to me already. News travels fast. When I came out of the liquor store and saw you there, I just figured you were trying to pin this on me. So I just blurted out the first thing that came into my head, wanting you to know that I didn't have anything to do with it." Bridgeport explained.

"Well then, who were these two or three people that informed you of the dead girl being found?" Sullivan inquired.

"Hell, I don't know their names. Just some people who I ran into in the last week or so. I swear, I couldn't tell you their names if my life depended on it!"

"It probably does," Sullivan quickly retorted.

Sullivan continued the interview by simply asking Bridgeport to account for his activities the previous day up to the time that he was confronted at the liquor store. Bridgeport stated he woke up around noon, ate, showered at his mother's house, and then went to his dad's tavern where he bartended from approximately 3pm until 8pm. Next he drove around Glen Burnie by himself, sipping on a fifth of Jack Daniels and smoking some hash. He was looking for something to do, somewhere to go. He did not see anyone he was interested in, so he went home and was in bed by 11pm. Bridgeport told Sullivan that the next thing he knew, it was 1or 2pm the following day. Like before, he took a shower and got something to eat. He sat at home, watching TV until around 8pm. Then, he drove down to Sal's Liquor Store to get a cold six-pack of beer. He denied seeing or talking to anyone during the time he was driving around the previous night. Sullivan asked Bridgeport the routes he took driving around Glen Burnie and also if he had driven out of town at anytime. Bridgeport said he could not remember where he drove, but denied leaving the limits of Glen Burnie. Bridgeport reiterated that no one was with him and he did not speak to anyone. He also denied having physical contact with anyone during the entire time he was cruising around from the time he left the bar until he went home to go to bed at approximately 11 pm.

Sullivan got more direct in his questioning. He was looking for an explanation regarding the corn stocks sticking out of the sides of his vehicle, the .22 caliber shell casings in the bed of the truck, and the necklace found in the seat of his truck. Bridgeport denied any knowledge of the things Sullivan asked him about, nor did he have any explanation for them. In what appeared to be a desperate attempt to come up with an explanation, Bridgeport mentioned leaving the key in the ignition of his unlocked truck, theorizing that someone could have taken it without his knowledge or consent. Sullivan ridiculed Bridgeport's explanation. It was ridiculous to think someone would steal his truck, and then turn around and return it back to Bridgeport's residence. At that point Bridgeport got angry and said the interview was over with as far as he was concerned. He then asked for an attorney. At that point, Sullivan had no alternative but to end the interview and lock Bridgeport up in the Poland County Jail.

Although Sullivan had placed Bridgeport under arrest, and ordered the truck impounded for safekeeping and evidentiary purposes, he was cautious. Sullivan felt he should get a search warrant for the truck before having it processed and examined. Therefore, he telephoned the county prosecutor explaining the situation to him. Sullivan asked the prosecutor to accompany him to the circuit court judge's residence in order to get a search warrant for the truck. After contacting the sleeping judge, they went to his residence, explained the events of the day, and requested a search warrant. The judge agreed with the request, confirming that there was plenty of probable cause for the search warrant. However, there was an incident that occurred that was both unexpected and unprofessional, and could have created a big problem in the entire investigation, had Sullivan not had a good relationship with the judge.

There was a knock on the front door. Sullivan's boss was standing there, accompanied by a local defense attorney who had been contacted by Bridgeport's mother. Bridgeport called her when he got his mandatory two phone calls. Sullivan's supervisor, Detective-In-Charge John Knapp, looked directly at Sullivan and spouted, "You have the wrong guy. He didn't do it."

Knapp gave his ridiculous opinion right in front of the judge who just agreed to issue the search warrant and who would soon rule in a probable cause hearing, making a determination if sufficient evidence existed to hold and charge Bridgeport with murder. Sullivan could not believe his ears.

Sullivan thought to himself, *What the hell was Knapp doing there in the first place, especially with Bridgeport's defense attorney? Why in God's name would he make a comment like that in front of the judge?*

The only thing Sullivan could conclude was that Knapp was even more stupid than Sullivan had originally believed him to be. It was either that or he was jealous that an apprehension had been made so quickly and Knapp had nothing to do with it. It was quickly becoming clear to Sullivan that Knapp was trying to sabotage the case for his own job security.

Sullivan pulled Knapp aside and told him in not-so-many kind words that he was *way* out of line. Sullivan further asked Knapp what he based an ignorant comment like that on. Knapp informed Sullivan that he spoke to Bridgeport (apparently after Sullivan had interrogated him), and Bridgeport pleaded that he did not do it. He even offered Knapp the stolen truck theory.

"What did you expect him to say? Did you really think he would confess?" Sullivan frustratingly wondered.

The history of Harold Sullivan and John Knapp went way back. They once had been close friends when they were troopers. However, once Sullivan made Detective Sergeant prior to Knapp (both were interviewing and testing for the same position), they quickly became adversaries. When Knapp did finally make Detective Sergeant, he was promoted by the famous state police "Peter Principle," which went as follows: If someone was incompetent or just downright lazy, you promoted them. The First Sergeant personally told Sullivan that he made Knapp the Detective-In-Charge over everyone else because he could not get Knapp to do his job. The First Sergeant stated the rationale behind his thinking was that he would at least get something out of Knapp, namely checking reports. He needed good detectives, like Sullivan, to do the real, important work. Initially, the Detective-In-Charge position was not a promotion, and did not really involve supervision over the other detectives. However, it soon changed and Knapp became the boss to all of the more-deserving detectives.

Finally, Knapp and the defense attorney left the judge's residence. Sullivan wasted no time in explaining to the judge the mistake in judgment by Knapp and apologized for the entire incident.

Sullivan proceeded to the facility where Bridgeport's pickup truck had been taken, in order to confer with the state police lab tech officers who were conducting the examination of the vehicle. As Sullivan walked into the garage area, he noticed the vehicle had been placed on a lift so the underneath of the vehicle could be observed and examined. He walked under the vehicle and began to observe it. No longer than five seconds went by when Sullivan noticed corn stocks and leaves still wedged between parts of the vehicle. Upon closer observation, he witnessed what appeared to be blood, flesh, and hair that was stuck and matted in various locations on the undercarriage of the vehicle. At first the detective could not believe his eyes. He was looking at the victim's face, matted in blood, flesh and hair, where she was ran over. Sullivan had seen a lot in his years as a trooper and a detective, but not many things were as gruesome as this. He suddenly had the overwhelming urge to get a hold of Bridgeport and beat him within an inch of his life. Unfortunately though, he knew he would have to take his frustrations out in other ways, namely drinking. Sullivan turned to this crutch more frequently than was advisable.

This murder took place several years before the technology of DNA was available, even though it was in the developmental stages. With the blood, flesh, and hair available, modern day detectives would have an open-and-shut case. Sullivan did not have it that easy.

After discussing details with the officers who were examining the truck for any and all physical evidence, Sullivan thought he would contact Joe Rallings in reference to the autopsy. He telephoned Rallings at the morgue, and let him know that he was on his way. Rallings advised him the autopsy had already been concluded. They agreed to meet at Jerry's Restaurant to have breakfast and discuss the case.

Only a seasoned cop could eat right after witnessing this kind of butchery. Sullivan felt this was simply business as usual. He thought about a few occasions when he had new troopers conducting on-the-job training with him. Once they began observing an autopsy, the new hires had to leave the room. There was one particular time where a truck driver was found in the sleeper of his cab, deceased. An autopsy had to be conducted to determine the cause of death in order to rule out any foul play. Sullivan brought two new troopers along for the ride. They were doing just fine until the saw came out. The top of the skull had to be removed in order to examine the brain. At that point, Sullivan heard the door open and close. He could hear both troopers outside, barfing their guts out. Sullivan thought to himself, *What a great way to initiate them into the wonderful world of their chosen vocation as Indiana State Police officers!*

CHAPTER SEVEN - A MILLION DOLLAR BOND?

Sullivan and Rallings met at the restaurant as planned. After a few minutes of small talk, Rallings informed Sullivan that the autopsy revealed several disturbing things. For starters, the victim had sexual intercourse (consensual?) around the time of death. She was shot thirteen times in the back, buttocks, and legs with a .22 caliber weapon, such as a rifle. Her back had carving type cuts on it as if someone had taken a knife or a sharp object and purposely carved diagrams in her back. Her face had been obliterated possibly from a tire running over it. Topping things off, something had been rammed up her rectum, which was about the size of a baseball bat. As unlikely and gruesome as it sounds, Rallings mentioned that most or all of the injuries occurred while the girl was still alive.

"Anything else, or is that about it?" Sullivan asked as he chewed his biscuits and gravy.

It is amazing how calm, cool, and collected someone can be when that person has been exposed to gruesome things over the years—things such as decapitations resulting from traffic accidents; suicides by unusual means like lying one's neck on the running chain of a chain saw; hanging themselves, and consequently defecating all over the room when the sphincter muscles gives way, etc. In reality, Sullivan was bothered and concerned at the gruesome and inhumane details Rallings had just related to him, but like all cops are expected to do, he forced himself to accept and live with the things he had to see and endure in his chosen profession. He learned to act like it did not bother him much; so he ended up keeping his emotions bottled up inside. After all, a police officer, especially a state police detective, has to put up an emotional shield that demonstrates professionalism, determination, good judgment, and nerves of steel in all situations he found himself in. This was the rule of thumb from the time he went 1041, until the time he went 1042 (police lingo for "going on duty" and "going off duty"). Psychologists have explained these experiences are part of the reasons for the high divorce, suicide, alcohol, and drug abuse rates among cops and the law enforcement community in general.

After eating a breakfast that would surely help clog his arteries, and smoking three well-deserved cigarettes, Sullivan left to head home for a quick shower and change of clothes. In big cases like this one, it was not unusual to work 24 or even 48 hours straight, before going off duty and getting some rest. The reason was simple, especially for a detective. It was his case and he was responsible for it. If something was not done properly or overlooked, it was his ass. There were certain things that had to be done and could not be postponed.

There was not another detective coming on duty the next shift to take over, so it went back to the inevitable conclusion: The detective assigned to the case stayed and made sure everything was done and done correctly.

After a quick shower, Sullivan headed to the prosecuting attorney's office in order to prepare for the probable cause hearing scheduled for that afternoon in Poland Circuit Court. However, before driving there, Sullivan decided he would try to contact Bridgeport's mother and talk to her. He wanted to get a timetable down about what time Bridgeport got home the previous night or early morning. It was important to speak with her and tie her to her story before she had a chance to talk to her son. They would surely compare their recollections, in order to get their stories straight and coordinated.

Sullivan knocked on the door and Mrs. Bridgeport answered. Someone apparently contacted her prior to this visit and informed her that her son had been arrested. She was dressed and acted as if she was expecting company. Knowing this type of family, it just seemed to Sullivan to be a little too polished. Sullivan introduced himself, and asked Mrs. Bridgeport if he could come in and talk to her for a few minutes. She reluctantly agreed, and he went in and sat down at the dining room table.

After some preliminary conversation, Sullivan asked her if she knew what time her son had gotten home and what time he had left. She said he had left in the evening about 4pm to go up to her ex-husband's tavern to work, and got home around 4:30am the next morning. Mrs. Bridgeport said she heard him drive up in his vehicle, slam the door shut, and enter the house. Mrs. Bridgeport mentioned that she glanced at her clock and also noticed that it was still dark outside. She knew nothing of her son's activities or who his friends were. In response to a direct question from Sullivan, she did not know anything about her son owning or having any guns or knives. Mrs. Bridgeport signed a "consent to search" form, and a search was conducted. Unfortunately, nothing of consequence was located that could have been associated with the murder investigation.

After leaving the Bridgeport residence, Sullivan proceeded to Jack Archer's office. Archer and Sullivan were a two-man team that knew and complimented one another very well. Archer was the prosecuting attorney while Sullivan acted as his sidekick and chief prosecuting witness. They were also personal friends who frequently socialized together, talking cases, while partaking of many cold Budweiser's. Sullivan was good at putting cases together in preparation for court trials. For his part, Archer was good at being the "loud, good ole boy, country lawyer," who had the uncanny ability of speaking the language of common, Southern Indiana people. He was very well liked, as was obvious by the fact he had been re-elected numerous times over the years. Archer's two strongest assets as an attorney were that he was unbelievably intelligent and was a natural talker. Archer would give one hell of a final argument off the cuff, unrehearsed, and unplanned.

Sullivan and Archer were busy discussing the details of the arrest and the case in general, as Archer was dictating the charging information to his secretary. All that was required in the upcoming probable cause hearing was testimony, mostly by Sullivan and possibly some by Rallings. There would be testimony by the two that there had been the crime of murder committed against a female person in Poland County. Sufficient evidence and information would be presented to the court to convince the judge that sufficient probable cause existed, indicating that Larry Bridgeport was the person who committed this crime.

By the time the charging information had been prepared it was almost noon. Therefore, the court hearing was postponed until 2pm. The judge brought the hearing to order and all parties took a seat, including Larry Bridgeport and his attorney Terry Lowell.

Lowell was a well-known, local attorney who had a well-deserved reputation as one of the best defense attorneys in the tri-state area. After the prosecutor briefly summarized why we were there, the judge turned to Bridgeport and asked him to identify himself, to which he did. Lowell stood up and advised the court he was representing Bridgeport.

Archer asked Detective Sullivan to take the stand. Archer began in earnest, starting the question-and-answer procedure to establish probable cause that the defendant, Larry Bridgeport, had committed the crime of murder. Archer began by asking Sullivan to give an account of his actions, and what he discovered, observed, and heard the morning the female body was discovered. Sullivan went through the details of the investigation one-by-one, one question after another, testifying to the evidence, circumstances, information and facts of his investigation that led to the discovery of the white-over-green El Camino and Larry Bridgeport. In a probable cause hearing there usually is not a whole lot of significance a defense attorney can ask a witness, but Lowell did his best and tried to put doubt in the judge's mind. Lowell asked Sullivan several questions such as:

Were there any witnesses who observed anything, including seeing Bridgeport with a female on the night in question?

Was the chrome strip positively identified as coming off of Bridgeport's El Camino?

Was any gun or cutting devise recovered?

Could the shell casings in the bed of the truck be identified as being fired from any particular gun, especially any gun associated with Bridgeport?

Could the corn stocks be identified as coming from the particular farm field the victim's body was located in?

Had the necklace found in the bed of the truck been identified as belonging to any particular person?

Were fingerprints recovered from the truck identifiable?

Could the blood, hair and flesh recovered from the underneath of the truck be identified as animal or human? If human, could it be identified as coming from any particular person?

Sullivan, who had much experience in testifying in court and had a reputation as being a very capable investigator and witness, routinely answered each question. Many of the above questions, and other inquiries made by the defense attorney, were answered by stating laboratory analysis had not been completed as of yet, and the victim had not been positively identified.

Rallings testified as to the results of the autopsy that were known thus far, and stated that the official cause of death was gunshots that penetrated the body, including two to the heart and one in each lung. Rallings was asked if analysis had been done on the body to determine if any kind of drugs were present in her body. He answered that tests were being done but were not yet completed. This basically concluded the probable cause hearing. The judge ruled there was sufficient probable cause to charge and hold Larry Bridgeport for first-degree murder. The defense attorney routinely asked for a reasonable bond so his client could be released. In return, the prosecuting attorney asked that the court set a one million dollar bond. Archer requested this for three reasons:

1) The monstrous nature of the murder.
2) The fact that Bridgeport might be a flight risk.
3) Bridgeport was a danger to society.

The judge quickly rejected the ridiculous one million dollar bond, but did set it at $250,000, an amount he apparently felt confident Bridgeport could not come up with.

After the hearing had concluded, Sullivan and Rallings met at Archer's office to discuss the case more and to establish a game plan as to what needed to be done to firm the case up. One conclusion was obvious and agreed upon—a lot of work needed to be done. The first order of business was to establish the identity of the female victim, then to connect her to Bridgeport in any and every way possible.

CHAPTER EIGHT - ARE TWO DUMMIES BETTER THAN ONE?

At this stage of the investigation, Sullivan had not slept in approximately thirty-six hours. His mental and physical capabilities were beyond diminished. The decision was made to finally go home and get some rest. He did not know how much sleep he would get considering that his kids would be running around the house, making noise; but he knew he had to try. As mentioned earlier, being a cop was not at all favorable to a healthy marriage.

Harry and his wife had been married for about ten years, only the first half being happy ones. Even though the last five years were trying, Harry tried to keep it together for the sake of his kids, whom he loved to a fault. In futile attempts to cope with their failing marriage, his wife reverted to a strict version of Christianity while Harry reverted to getting liquored up as often as possible. Drinking certainly was not an asset to a crumbling marriage or to the duties of a state police detective, but Harry managed the best he could with what he had.

Harry attempted to find a middle ground by joining his wife at church, but it did not take as he hoped and even prayed it would. He observed the speaking in tongues, putting oil on people's foreheads, and shoving them to the ground in healing ceremonies. Harry sometimes wondered if they were going to come out with poisonous snakes some night and handle them as proof of their faith. To Harry, all of these experiences were suspicious in nature. However, the straw that broke the camel's back was when on one occasion a person whom had been a prime suspect in a bank robbery Harry had investigated came up to him and asked to escort the detective up to the alter to pray with the preacher in order to be born again. Harry certainly was not an atheist or even agnostic. He did not have the nerve to be. After all, if someone does not believe in a higher power, the absolute best that can occur is when that person dies, the lights simply go out and the person was right. The worst is, of course, eternal damnation in the fiery pits of Hell. Harry did not want any part of that, so he believed Jesus was The Son of God, he just did not practice nor was he a good boy.

It did not take long to figure out that this particular type of religion was not his cup o' tea, even though he was raised in a relatively conservative church. It appeared more and more obvious that once his wife began attending this Pentecostal church, the further and further apart they went.

It should be noted that at this particular time the state police did not have overtime. There were many more applications versus the amount of openings available. Because of that, it was considered to be an honor to be a state policeman in the state of Indiana. Considering this fact, overtime pay (time-and-a-half pay, anyway) was not even a consideration. It got so bad that if an officer worked on his regular day off, he *might* get a day off later on to make up for it, only at the department's discretion.

After about six hours of desperately-needed sleep, Sullivan was back at it. The first order of business was getting the victim identified. He checked missing person's flyers and checked local, county, state, and federal authorities with no success. Considering where the murder occurred and the body was found, his intuition told him it was probably someone local. He just could not understand why the young woman had not been reported missing by her family. Rumors were running wild in regards to the identity of the girl and what were the circumstances that led to her death that night.

Sullivan heard that one of the girls who might have been present was a girl named Sherry Furrows, who was a known drug user who got unusually crazy when high. Sullivan proceeded to look her up and see if she had any information reference the murder. After locating Sherry, he asked her if she knew anything about the murder or the identity of the girl. Furrows played dumb. Sullivan was unsure if she was telling the truth or not. Sherry said she had been "shacked up" in a local motel, with a local boy the night and early morning of the murder. Sullivan later checked with the motel owner and the boy she was allegedly with. They corroborated her story.

To have a better chance of positively identifying the deceased girl, later on that same day, Rallings contacted Sullivan and asked him what he thought about the idea of putting pictures of the girl's jewelry in the newspaper. Sullivan thought that was a great idea. In no time at all, a state police narcotics officer named Lenny McCam made a surprising and unexpected statement. Looking at the jewelry, he informed Rallings he knew whose jewelry it was. He stated without hesitation the jewelry belonged to a girl he recently spoke with named Beth Cowens. He mentioned he noticed the jewelry on her when he spoke to her previously. Rallings immediately telephoned the girl's mother, Vivian Cowens, and was asked to come to the state police post to take a look at the jewelry. Vivian Cowens immediately came to the post, and with dread, positively identified the jewelry as being her daughter's, Beth Cowens. After she regained her composure, she stated she had not seen or heard from Beth in two or three days. Sullivan then asked Mrs. Cowens to describe her daughter, and her description fit the murdered girl to a tee. Mrs. Cowens brought in a picture of her daughter, at Sullivan's request. Sullivan believed based on the picture brought in that they were one and the same. Sullivan believed he had finally identified the poor girl who had been raped, tortured, and murdered. Now, he had to convict the lowlife piece-of-shit who committed this horrendous act. Sullivan's intuition told him that Bridgeport was probably not involved in this crime by himself, even though the cover-up of the crime was sloppy and one might even say, nonexistent. Bridgeport surely had one or more accomplices. After all, two dummies are better than just one…right?

In his conversation with the mother of Beth Cowens, Sullivan was somewhat surprised at the apparent lack of knowledge Mrs. Cowens had about the activities of her daughter. Routine questions were asked of Mrs. Cowens.

Who were Beth's friends?
Who were the boys Beth was recently dating?
When was the last time you spoke to her?
What were her habits?
Why wasn't she reported to the police as missing?

Mrs. Cowens answered the last time she spoke to Beth was shortly after 12pm on the day she disappeared. She confessed Beth had gotten kind of wild and she could not do anything with her. Mrs. Cowens revealed she had not reported her missing because Beth had done this sort of thing on several occasions. She would disappear for a day or two at a time, but always returned back home. When she would ask Beth where she had been or what she had been doing, Beth always answered that she had spent the last day or two with some of her girlfriends at their houses. Of course, Mrs. Cowens could not offer one single name of her daughter's girlfriends. Sullivan already figured the answer when he asked her what boys Beth might have been seeing. It was obvious that she took little to no interest in Beth's life, what she was doing, or who she was doing it with. This was probably one of the main reasons Beth was running the streets at fourteen years-old, and doing things that she should not have been doing at any age. This was, unfortunately, one of the major factors leading to her untimely and gruesome death.

Now that the identity of the victim had been tentatively made, Sullivan knew his work had really just begun. He had to get to the bottom of exactly what happened in that cornfield, who was involved, and what part anyone who was there played in Beth Cowens's murder.

CHAPTER NINE - FAMILY RITUALS

      The time finally arrived for a couple of days off. Sullivan thought he had the investigation well in hand enough to take time away. He believed the urgent details had been taken care of. Unfortunately, the long, drawn-out, grinding part of the investigation lay in front of him. Sullivan really *had* to have this time off in order to be mentally ready for the obstacles that he knew he would face in this investigation.

      It was Friday night and that usually meant eating out, most likely at Godfathers Pizza in Morganville. Harry, his wife Belinda, and the two kids, Holly and Brian, loaded up in the state police vehicle and headed out for a big evening on the town. The use of the state police vehicle while off duty was one of the benefits of being a state police officer.

      Little was said between Harry and his wife on the way to the restaurant. Belinda usually asked very little about his work. Truth be told, she really did not care very much. Her main interests in life were two-fold—going to Morganville on weekends to visit her family, and attending church every Sunday. Neither of those options interested Harry in the slightest. He felt her family was about as white trash as white trash got. He attempted the church thing but it did not take for whatever reason. Harry's life revolved around four things during the last few years—lifting weights, his kids, his job, and indulging in alcoholic beverages every chance he got. Those were the only things that made him feel good about his miserable life.

      Harry had been a physical fitness guy most of his adult life, consisting primarily of weightlifting, running, and playing basketball. His desire to lift weights came mostly from frustration when he was a skinny kid whom every bully could humiliate. The fear of getting his ass handed to him drove Harry to achieve size and strength. When he became a state police officer, he decided he was going to make himself bigger and stronger. This way, rather than getting his ass kicked, as he did when he was a kid, he could now be the one who was doing the ass-kicking! He did get relatively big, carrying two hundred and thirty pounds on his six-foot frame. Thankfully, Harry seldom had to use his physical capacity in his line of work as much as he thought he would. People would usually take one look at this imposing figure and decide against trying anything.

      After an evening of eating pizza and drinking two pitchers of beer (Harry, not Belinda), he and the family returned home. The children went to their rooms to do whatever kids did. Belinda went into the bedroom to read *The Bible* and pray before she went to bed. Meanwhile, Harry went downstairs to the basement's family room to watch television. This was the standard Friday night ritual when Harry was home. Usually, around midnight, he went upstairs to bed. Like most men in their mid-thirties, Harry was hornier than a three-peckerd goat. To say he had a hard-on a cat couldn't scratch would not be an understatement.

Even though he did not have a fulfilling relationship with Belinda didn't mean he wanted to ignore his biological needs. With that, he slid into bed, ready for some Friday night action! He moved close to Belinda and began rubbing her with the thought of getting her in the mood. Being the smooth, romantic talker he was, he tried for a little flattery, even though he knew it was all bullshit.

"Honey, you looked awfully good tonight," he lied.

"Leave me alone. I'm tired and don't feel good. I ate too much," Belinda countered.

"I've missed you all week. I just thought we could spend some time together here," Harry reasoned.

"Not tonight. I have to get up early in the morning to go to Mom's," Belinda stated, shooting Harry's heartfelt advances down in burning flames.

Harry knew if he protested enough she would probably give in, but it just was not worth it to him. To avoid an argument, he simply responded that it was fine, rolled over, and went to sleep…again, with a hard-on a cat couldn't scratch.

Hell, she'd just lie there anyway, acting like she was doing me a big favor. It would be about the equivalent of having sex with a comatose person anyway, so why bother? Harry thought to himself as he rolled over.

Like most Saturdays, Belinda left early in the morning for her mother's house in Morganville, taking Holly with her and leaving Brian with Harry. This being summertime meant it was time to mow the yard. Brian ran off to play with some of the neighborhood boys. However, this Saturday was busier than usual, and Harry was on the phone most of the day. He was receiving calls from other law enforcement officials, or the public, mostly in reference to the Beth Cowens murder investigation. Did they not realize the lawn was almost out of control?

That was another thing about being a state policeman in Indiana. They were *required* to have a published phone number, so they would be available to the public if someone wanted or needed to call them. In other words, they were everybody's public servant and private police officers. If citizens had a question, needed advice, or had a problem, the governor of the great state of Indiana and superintendent of the state police wanted officers available to assist them. After all, that was what the state paid cops the big bucks for! That kind of stuff got old very quickly. Harry often thought to himself if he had an IQ above a chimp, he would do something else for a living.

On Sunday, Belinda took (forced) the kids to church. Once she returned, the whole family went out for Sunday brunch. As you might be able to decipher, dining out was the only activity the family ever did together as a group. Later on, once the kids were in bed, it was time for another weird ritual…Harry finally got him some. On that wonderful "day of rest," Belinda would usually relent and take fifteen to twenty minutes out of her pious day to give her gracious husband the joys of carnal bliss. Oh, how wonderful it was to be a happily married man with a loving wife on a sensuous Sunday evening!

CHAPTER TEN - P.E. TEACHER, PREACHER, OR A COP

On Monday morning around eight it was "3582 Morganville, 1041," which meant Detective Harry Sullivan was signing on to work. He was now officially on duty, ready to protect and serve. It was just another day of him continuing in his chosen career as a crime fighter and a solver of murders and other various forms of mayhem and mischief. Yes, Poland county, and the entire state of Indiana for that matter, could sigh a sigh of relief, because Detective Sullivan was on the job!

The first order of business was a radio message to the detective that he was supposed to proceed, sooner rather than later, to meet with his superior officer at the state police post. This was the same simpleton who had come to the judge's house while Sullivan was attempting to get a search warrant for Bridgeport's truck. It was there where he informed Sullivan, in front of the judge, that Sullivan had arrested and incarcerated the wrong man for the most heinous murder that had ever been committed in Poland County. That was the absolute last thing Sullivan wanted to hear on a Monday morning—advice and counsel from that idiot! It took all of the self-control that Sullivan possessed not to just disregard the order. However, like a good soldier, he proceeded to the post as instructed. It was in the back office of the criminal investigation division where Detective-in-Charge John Knapp was waiting for him. Knapp was his usual self-serving and arrogant self.

"Well, are you sure you've got the right guy in jail? We don't want to screw this up. This is a big case that has gotten a lot of publicity. Even the brass in Indianapolis has their eye on us!" Knapp informed Sullivan.

"Yeah, I've got the right guy in jail. Is that all?" Sullivan curtly asked.

Since he probably did not have much to do, Knapp wanted to discuss the case further. It took everything Sullivan had to even tolerate being around him. The last thing he wanted to do was sit down and chit-chat about a case with someone who was a lousy detective. Sullivan advised him he had a lot of work to do, and really wanted to get going on it. Knapp relented and asked Sullivan to keep him posted.

Sullivan felt the evidence had Beth connected to Bridgeport's truck. That much was obvious. However, he knew the connection to Bridgeport on the night of the murder had to be made. One challenge was that a gun had never been recovered. Adding to that was the fact that Bridgeport asked for an attorney before the gun issue could even be pursued. Also, a search of Bridgeport's mother's house produced nothing as far as a weapon was concerned. Rumors were spreading, so it was imperative that questions concerning the case, including "what happened" and "who was involved," be answered ASAP. The first thing Sullivan decided to do was locate and talk with local, young people whom he knew. Most of these individuals had problems with the law over drugs and similar issues. Generally speaking, they were sucking up perfectly good oxygen.

The first person Sullivan looked up was a Joe Rogers, who usually cruised around town just about every single night. Rogers was familiar with just about everyone in town and usually knew what was going on. It was only about one in the afternoon, so Sullivan knew that Rogers was probably still sleeping in his upstairs apartment located in a big, older house owned by his father. Sullivan knocked on the severely paint-deprived door. It seemed like damn-near twenty minutes went by until he finally heard activity inside the apartment. A large canine began barking loudly. The door opened and there stood Joe Rogers in his bath robe, rubbing the sleep out of his eyes. His eyes focused on the detective.

"What do you want this early in the day, Sullivan?" Rogers wondered.

Sullivan reminded him it was after noon, and then asked to step inside so he could ask him a few questions. Rogers reluctantly agreed since he did not want Indiana's finest riding him in the future. Sullivan sat down at the filthy kitchen table and proceeded to tell Rogers why he was there.

"Joe, I guess you heard about the murder that happened a few days ago."

Rogers nodded 'yes.'

"Well, I arrested Tater Bridgeport for it, and we found out that the victim was Beth Cowens. I was wondering if you were out and about the night the murder was committed. If so, do you recall whom you observed or talked to on that particular night? In addition, I was wondering if you knew of or heard about any association between Tater and Beth."

"Yeah, I was out that night, hanging out at the IGA parking lot most of the night, talking to different people. I don't know Beth Cowens, but I do know Bridgeport; but I don't remember seeing him that night."

Sullivan felt Rogers was being truthful because he spoke to him before on a range of issues, and he had always been truthful during those occasions. Rogers did mention that he heard plenty of rumors, such as devil worship, girls ganging up on Beth, torture, and gang-rape by several unnamed guys. He continued, stating he heard the rumor that she was possibly murdered over a drug deal gone sour. Rogers also mentioned that he heard that Bridgeport had been involved in selling quite a bit of drugs lately. Sullivan thanked him for the information and asked Rogers to contact him if he heard anything further.

Detective Harold Sullivan was not necessarily the sharpest knife in the drawer, but he was considered a very hard-working, hard-nosed criminal investigator. This was in part because Sullivan possessed the five qualities that he considered crucial in order to be a successful investigator:

1) Determination
2) Being nosey and somewhat bothersome
3) Personal responsibility to victims and their families
4) Personal pride in the job
5) Intimidation (when necessary)

These qualities were developed over the years in his personality as a reflection of what he had seen, heard, and participated in. One thing he learned the hard way was that people, particularly the criminal element, were the same. It did not matter if someone was an officer in a large metropolitan area or in the rural areas of Southern Indiana. Most of the scumbags that were questioned lied, or at the very least, bent the truth to benefit them. Everyone was out for old number one at the expense of everyone else. Greed ran rampant when it came to money, personal possessions, drugs, alcohol, and sex.

Sullivan was positive he had arrested the right person in Bridgeport, but strongly believed Bridgeport was not alone when the act took place. Experience and knowledge accumulated over the years told him the carving on the back and the ramming of something up the rectum of Beth were acts even an extremely deranged person would not usually commit by himself. Sullivan knew if he wanted a successful conclusion to this case in court, he was going to have to:

1) Provide an accurate description of what actually happened out in that cornfield.
2) Be able to name everyone involved and the levels of participation.
3) Discover the reason or reasons (motive) why this particular cruel and inhumane crime was committed.

Although Sullivan had made a quick (and extremely lucky) apprehension, he knew his investigation had really just begun. The first thing he had to do was put Tater Bridgeport and Beth Cowens together, particularly on that night. He figured he had enough evidence to convict Bridgeport's truck, but he had to put Bridgeport in it at the time and location of the murder.

Sullivan felt the extreme pressure and responsibility that someone feels being in charge of an investigation such as this. Based on previous experiences, he knew that if things went right, he would probably not get the amount of credit he deserved. If things went wrong, Sullivan would almost certainly get all of the blame. Such is the vocation he chose.

As Sullivan had humorously, but truthfully, told people over the years, when he was young he knew he did not have the intelligence to be a doctor or a lawyer. That left him with three "P" choices—a P.E. teacher, a preacher, or a policeman. He knew he would make an extremely poor preacher. He did not believe he would make much of a teacher either. So, that left the last option available.

Sullivan did not feel someone had to be a rocket scientist to be a cop. The work did not look too physically strenuous, unless you call drinking coffee and eating donuts physically demanding. Although the pay was not spectacular by any measurable standard, he felt it was good enough to live a normal, middle class life, and that was good enough for him. The job description that made Sullivan a little hesitant in reference to his choice of becoming a police officer was the danger element. As a kid he was basically a chicken shit who just about anyone could beat up. Like most people, he had plenty of hang-ups and faults (probably more than most), but he knew he had to do *something* for a living. He certainly did not enjoy physical labor, nor was he good at it anyway. In his mind, that left one alternative…becoming a cop.

CHAPTER ELEVEN - INFORMANTS AND COMPLIMENTS

Detective Sullivan was on his way to Poland Circuit Court for a hearing requested by Bridgeport's attorney. The hearing was scheduled to cover several different issues, such as requesting a change of venue and a motion for supplemental discovery (the process of gaining access to the prosecution's evidence). Sullivan had to testify as to the extensive publicity of the case, especially in the Poland County area. People around there were simply not accustomed to a murder occurring in one of their towns. Consequently, a change of venue was granted for the case to be moved to Harrison County. The motion for discovery was routinely granted. All reports, evidence, and statements were ordered turned over to the defense as soon as they became available.

Looking at Tater Bridgeport's upbringing, it was not surprising that he was not a stellar citizen or a man of the cloth. However, it was a far leap from being a doper and petty criminal to becoming the person who could commit a heinous crime such as this. He had been a troublemaker since junior high, being involved in various scrapes in school and with the law. His mother appeared to be a decent person, who tried to raise him the best she knew how. Bridgeport's mother and father had been divorced since he was a child, so the upbringing, for the most part, fell to her. His father was thought to be on the fringe of the criminal element. It was suspected over the years that he was involved in gambling, stolen property, and the sale of drugs. So, in this case, the apple obviously did not fall far from the tree. Tater was, unfortunately, influenced by his father's conduct and the environment of that lifestyle. He apparently had little or no guidance or discipline in his early life, which seemed to feed on itself. In this particular instance, the lack of those attributes created a monster just waiting to be unleashed.

Beth Cowens was obviously raised in an environment that was far from ideal. She had several siblings, two of which were deceased as a result of tragic accidents. Her father was mostly uneducated and worked sparingly. Her mother usually had her hand close to a whiskey bottle. Beth was raised in an economically deprived situation, with little or no guidance and discipline. She was allowed to run the streets at about twelve years-old. Beth was a physically-developed, attractive girl. This naturally made her appear to be older than her chronological age. She missed school almost as much as she attended. It was not at all uncommon for her to be suspended from school due to her actions. Simply put, she was a kid who fell through the cracks. Did this prove to invite tragedy, ending her life in a violent manner at an early age?

Again, rumors regarding the details, motives, and manner of this murder were running rampant—everything from devil worship, witchcraft, revenge killing, and a gangbang that got out of control were a few of the theories being circulated around town. Sullivan was for sure Tater Bridgeport was the ringleader of everything.

The next and most important thing Sullivan had to do was put Bridgeport and Beth Cowens together, especially on the night of the murder. Sullivan received a message to contact a local scumbag whom he had dealings with in the past named Billy Most. Billy was a guy who was always out and about, and usually had a line on everything that was going on.

Sullivan telephoned Billy to schedule a meeting with him to inquire what he knew about this murder. The first thing Billy wanted to know was what was in it for him. Sullivan reminded Billy that he was already in debt to the detective for helping him out of a few scrapes in the past for things, such as providing alcohol to minors, selling stolen property, and a statutory rape allegation involving a girl who was fifteen years-old at the time. Also, Sullivan had "leaned" on a couple of local thugs who were threatening to beat Billy within an inch of his life for not paying certain debts that they claimed he owed them. Sullivan did not do these favors out of the kindness of his heart. He did them because Billy was usually a great source of information. Every street cop knew it was wise to have a few sources of information like Billy Most available, especially during times like this. The life of a detective was always one of compromise, rationalization, and the benefits outweighing the costs. Billy, after deciding it was to his benefit to tell the detective what he knew, gave Sullivan the break he had been looking for.

"Okay, I'll tell you what I heard, but you didn't get this information from me. I was hanging out the other night, talking to a guy and his girlfriend. They mentioned that they saw Beth riding around town with Tater in his truck the night she was killed. She was sitting close to him as he drove through the city park. Those bright street lights must have been on, which allowed them to get a good look 'em. I heard that Bridgeport had been fuckin' Beth for quite awhile, and that they'd been using and selling a lot of grass."

"Who told you they saw Beth and Tater together that night?" Sullivan questioned Billy.

"Joe Broshears and Linda Selbey," Billy quickly answered.

Sullivan could hardly hide his elation that he just received case-breaking information. He hoped it was accurate and if so, he could convince Broshears and Selbey to give him the same information in written statements.

Sullivan contacted Joe Broshears and asked him and his girlfriend to meet him at the local Indiana State Police Post. He decided to take statements from them separately. The written statement of Joe Broshears was taken by Detective Sullivan as follows:

"Last Tuesday evening around nine o'clock, I was parked at the city park with my girlfriend, Linda Selbey. We were parked right next to the road that runs through the park, facing the road, directly under a street light, just talking. I noticed Larry "Tater" Bridgeport driving by at a low rate of speed in his white-over-green El Camino. Sitting very close to him in the seat was Beth Cowens. I got a good look at them when they drove by and mentioned it to my girlfriend. She saw them too, and mentioned that Beth was not very old, but at the same time, did not know exactly how old she was. She said she thought Beth was 'jailbait.' I made the comment that Bridgeport would break her in right, and even made the comment, 'Old enough to bleed, old enough to butcher!' Linda did not find that very funny. As it turned out, that was really a weird thing to say, considering what I heard a few days later concerning the horrible things that were done to Beth on that night. I knew who Beth Cowens was because I had noticed her walking up and down the streets lately, but did not know her personally. I do know Larry Bridgeport, although we do not run around together. I just know him well enough to talk to him when I see him around town."

Although it was very short, Broshears's statement was obviously very important to the case since he witnessed Bridgeport and Cowens together on the night of the murder. Sullivan then took a written statement from Linda Selbey, which contained the same basic information that was in Broshears's statement. Sullivan now had concrete information, not only connecting Beth to Bridgeport's truck on the night she was later murdered, but information connecting her with Bridgeport himself on that very same night.

After taking the statements, Sullivan proceeded to Morganville for the monthly law enforcement meeting. This consisted of meeting with officers and investigators of other police agencies in the tri-state area. Heading the meetings was a highly-regarded, retired FBI agent named Ben Gannon. The first thing Gannon did after bringing the meeting to order was compliment Sullivan on his quick apprehension in the Beth Cowens murder.

"I think Detective Sullivan should be complimented on one of the finest pieces of police work I have seen in my lifetime. It is my understanding that Officer Sullivan had a suspect in custody based on some very quick and innovative police work in this particular murder. This all took place on the same day the body was discovered and even before the victim had been identified. This kind of investigative police work makes the entire law enforcement community look professional, and holds us all to a very high standard of accomplishment."

Sullivan really appreciated this compliment, especially considering the individual it was coming from. He believed it was moments like this that really made the headaches, dangers, pressures, bad hours, and low pay worth it. It was then that he thought to himself maybe he would make it to heaven after all. Surely the good things he did in life outweighed the bad ones. Maybe he would slip into a corner of heaven since the preponderance of evidence was in his favor.

After the meeting, Sullivan went to his favorite watering hole for a few (several) beers. The Bobtail Inn was considered the most respectful tavern in the small town where he resided. Making things even more attractive to him was the fact that he very seldom ran into anyone there who caused him trouble. Sullivan had enough of that at work; he sure did not need it when he was off the clock. Everyone there knew him and knew what he did for a living. Most of the people who frequented this establishment were friends or acquaintances. The owner was a personal friend of Sullivan's, which made him feel like home when he was seated at the bar.

Sullivan ordered the first of many beers. The bartender mentioned to him he had not seen him in a few days but knew why. All anyone had to do was read the newspaper or watch the local news to know why Detective Harry Sullivan had been conspicuously absent lately. Although the bartender knew Sullivan did not like to discuss his business at the bar, Joe did make a comment loud enough for most of the nearby customers to hear.

"Good work, Harry. I'm glad to see you locked the son-of-a-bitch up who did that to that poor girl. Whenever I first heard about it, I knew you'd catch him. I just didn't think even you could do it as quickly as you did!"

The rest of the bar patrons all said "here-here," and gave Sullivan a generous round of applause. Harry did not have to pay for a single beer on this particular evening, which he and his budget very much appreciated.

Since he had been gone a lot lately, Sullivan knew he should head home. The problem was that other than seeing his kids, he really did not have very many reasons to go home. Harry already knew all too well the harsh reality that his wife cared very little for him. Harry was just a meal ticket to her. She did enjoy the respect she thought she received from the locals, being Detective Harry Sullivan's wife.

Belinda's enjoyments in life consisted of going to Morganville as often as she could to visit her family, attending church, and frequenting yard sales and resale shops in the area. Harry certainly was not the best-looking guy to come down the pike, and had little luck with the fairer sex. He occasionally thought about straying, but his sense of morality would not allow him to do it. When it came to sex with his wife, Harry felt he was definitely deprived. If he got some action once a week, he was practically counting his lucky stars!

On this particular night, Harry closed the Bobtail Inn down and got a cold six-pack to go. He carefully (as much as possible) drove home and pulled into the driveway. Harry turned off the motor but kept the radio on. He pulled out a George Jones cassette tape from the glove box and inserted it into the stereo. It was there where he proceeded to finish off his six-pack. He cried during the last beer. The effect of the alcohol and his miserable homelife got the best of him. It was in the car that Harry awoke to hear birds chirping outside while the tape continued to replay some of Harry's favorites about women who did good men wrong, which Harry felt matched his life to a tee.

CHAPTER TWELVE - INQUISITIONS WITH SCUMBAGS

Sullivan followed up on every lead he had, but most either ended up being a dead end, or the information very seldom could be substantiated. Bridgeport apparently was not saying anything to anyone except his attorney. No one in the jail population was volunteering anything that might be helpful. Getting information from inmates was always a treacherous way of getting it anyway. The inmate always had an ulterior motive for providing it, and the information could very seldom be confirmed. What Sullivan did not know was if there were more people involved in the murder. His experience was that someone involved in a crime usually could not keep their mouth shut and eventually told someone something.

Sullivan was informed that Vance Furrows wanted to speak with him. Mr. Furrows was the father of Sherry Furrows. She was the original girl that Sullivan originally thought might have been the victim. When he located and questioned her, she stated she knew nothing about the murder.

Sullivan met with her father as he requested. Mr. Furrows had obviously been drinking and appeared enraged when Sullivan spoke with him. He was furious at Sullivan because he questioned his seventeen year-old daughter and did not get permission from her father. Sullivan attempted to explain the circumstances that he spoke to her as a witness, not a suspect. That did not satisfy Mr. Furrows. He went on and on with his ranting. This was just some of the crap a police officer sometimes had to deal with. Sullivan was accustomed to it. He finally had his fill of listening to Vance Furrows and told him to shut his mouth, go home, or he would lock him up on the spot for public intoxication. As Furrows walked away, he muttered something about being a taxpayer and would get Sullivan fired. Sullivan thought to himself, *If an idiot like that could get me fired, the job wasn't worth having anyway!*

Later on that day, Sullivan received an anonymous phone call. The unknown caller simply stated, *You need to check out Harry Seasons.* Seasons was a well-known, pimply-faced bum who was known to be a thief, dope seller, and sex pervert. He had been arrested several times for various offenses including theft, sale of controlled substances, child molesting, rape, and attempted rape. Sullivan arrested him a couple of times himself but never knew of him to be particularly violent…just a scumbag.

Sullivan did think it was possible that Seasons could have been involved in the horrific acts that were perpetrated on Beth Cowens. However, he did not believe that Seasons would act alone—an additional person or persons almost *had* to be involved. Before he approached Seasons himself,

Sullivan felt he should talk to a few people first. These were people whom he went to in the past for information. He would ask if they heard any rumors about the murder and Harry Seasons's possible involvement.

Sullivan contacted the Poland County socialite, Joe Rogers, to find out what he knew about Harry Seasons and his association with Tater Bridgeport. Rogers said he did not personally know of Bridgeport and Seasons running together, and that he never observed them associating with one another as a rule. Rogers did mention that Seasons was the first person he thought of once he found out about the murder. Based on what he gathered, Rogers felt that if it involved rape or weird sex acts, it fit Seasons's motive of operandi perfectly.

Sullivan then contacted the rat, Billy Most, to find out what he knew regarding Seasons and his associations with Bridgeport or Beth Cowens. Most essentially said the same thing Rogers spoke about earlier. He did not know anything about Seasons being associated with Bridgeport or Beth Cowens, but said Seasons was one of the first persons he would think of when it came to rape or sodomy.

Sullivan had nothing he could hang his hat on when it came to questioning Seasons. He figured it would most likely be a waste of time to question or interrogate him, but did not know what else to do. The only things Sullivan had to tie Seasons to Bridgeport or Beth was the anonymous phone call he received, and Seasons's history of sex-related offenses. Sullivan decided to talk to Seasons as a witness; first using a low-key approach:

1) Asking what he heard reference the murder.
2) His thoughts about who may have been involved.
3) His knowledge of and relationship with Tater Bridgeport and Beth Cowens.

Sullivan knew Seasons's hangout was the Big Track Lounge. He wanted to catch him by surprise, so he drove to the Big Track Lounge and ordered a beer, waiting for Seasons to arrive. Sullivan did not mind that part, of course. Drinking alcohol was something that was almost as familiar to him as breathing. Sullivan knew Seasons's routine was to come into the tavern every day, around six in the evening. Sure enough, at six sharp, Harry Seasons walked through the door and sat down at the bar. Sullivan got up from his bar stool and went down to the end of the bar so he could be in close proximity to Seasons.

"What are you drinking?" Sullivan asked.

Seasons appeared surprised at Detective Sullivan suddenly sitting next to him.

"Uh, I'll have a shot of Kessler's with a Bud Light chaser."

Sullivan gave the order to the bartender, and placed a five dollar bill on the bar to pay for the drinks. Sullivan suggested they sit in a corner booth so they could have some privacy. Seasons begrudgingly agreed and they walked over to a corner booth in the poorly-lit bar room.

In Sullivan's opinion, Seasons was a pimply-faced puke that he could not stand. Being in his vicinity really made Sullivan feel he was earning his paycheck on that particular day. Seasons would lie to you when the truth was easier and more beneficial to him. Sullivan started the conversation by getting right to the crux of the situation.

"So, what did you hear regarding the Beth Cowens murder?"

Seasons got defensive right off the bat. "Hey man, you don't think I had anything to do with that do you? Fuck no. I wouldn't be involved in something like that!"

"Well, what have you heard"? Sullivan inquired.

"Really nothing, man…just talk and crazy rumors. I know Tater and I really can't believe he would be involved in something like that. I didn't even know the Cowens girl. She was nothing but jailbait to me."

"Since when did the age matter to you Harry? Everybody knows you'll fuck 'em from eight to eighty!" Sullivan exclaimed.

"Not anymore." Seasons lied. "I've learned my lesson!"

Sullivan knew he was not going to get Seasons to admit anything, but he did want to pull his chain a little.

"Well, I heard from a reliable source not only did you know about it, but you were right in the middle of it! Why don't you come down to the police post with me and give me a full statement? I will tell the prosecutor that you cooperated. Hell, Bridgeport probably did most of it anyway, didn't he?"

In reality, knowing Seasons's background, Sullivan believed the opposite was most likely true. Sullivan then attempted a little reverse-psychology.

"What the hell could you do? He had a .22 rifle and you were probably just stuck there! He probably would've shot you too if you hadn't gone along with him."

Sullivan was afraid this ploy was not going to work with Seasons, considering the number of run-ins he experienced with law enforcement. He was used to this type of questioning. Seasons was red-faced, scared, and at the same time, pissed off, but trying to hide his emotions.

"Man, I had absolutely nothing to do with that! I don't even know where I was at that night, but I sure as hell know I wasn't in that cornfield having anything to do with fucking or killing Beth Cowens!" Seasons exclaimed.

"Well, I guess since you had absolutely nothing to do with it and don't know anything about it, you wouldn't mind taking a polygraph test, right?" Sullivan wondered.

"Hell no! You're trying to frame me! I know how those lie detectors work anyway. They're not reliable and you can't use the results in court anyway. The cops just use them to trick people," Seasons finished.

With that said, Sullivan knew he was wasting his time. The conversation was coming to an esmsmsmmsnd. As he got up to leave, Sullivan had one final comment for Seasons to mull over.

"I know you had something to do with this. You better come clean before I put it together myself. If I figure it out before you tell me the truth, I'll personally see to it that you're charged with the death penalty! You'd better think about that," Sullivan threatened.

Sullivan felt sure the little puke was lying through his teeth. Considering that he received an anonymous call that led him to Seasons, he knew someone else knew or suspected something. When Seasons refused to take the polygraph test, that made him seem even guiltier. Sullivan was very confident that Seasons was hiding something, and not telling the truth about his knowledge or involvement in the murder of Beth Cowens.

Sullivan was afraid if he could not get more concrete evidence about what happened at the murder site and who was involved, with good attorneys, Bridgeport just might get off. Sullivan felt the chances of a conviction with the truck and accompanying circumstantial evidence would most likely be sufficient. However, with no witnesses to the actual crime and the circumstantial evidence the state had to go on, a murder conviction was anything but a foregone conclusion. Sullivan never investigated a case with as few concrete leads and evidence to follow up on. It was as if no one knew anything, or if they did, they certainly were not saying anything. Sullivan pretty well knew the defense would try to convince the jury of four points:

1) Sullivan ran an incompetent investigation.
2) Sullivan zeroed in on Bridgeport and turned a blind eye to any other possible suspects.
3) That Beth was a little tramp who used drugs and had sex with anybody.
4) That someone could have stolen Bridgeport's truck, committed the act, and then brought the vehicle back in order to pin the murder on Bridgeport.

A defense attorney's job is to convince one or more jurors that there is reasonable doubt, in order to give them an out or excuse to find the defendant not guilty of the crime he/she was accused of. The approach of defense attorneys are pretty much the same. They want to see what evidence the state has against their client, and then dig up people who will testify to what they want them to testify to. This usually involves an alibi. Defense attorneys might try explaining away or convincing the jury the evidence presented by the state was doubtful or unreliable.

The defense does not have to prove any of their theories. They simply just have to give an explanation, regardless of how farfetched it is. They present to the jury what *could* have happened, which would explain away the state's theory of the case and the existing evidence. The defense attorney's main goal is to explain away the testimony, evidence, and theories of the state's case. Most of the time, jurors do not want the responsibility of convicting a person of murder, which usually means life in prison or death. Therefore, sometimes a jury does not really need much of a reason to acquit a person, or at least find them guilty of a lesser included offense.

In the state of Indiana, a defense attorney has the right to enter lesser included offenses for the jurors to deliberate on, just in case they do not have the balls to convict the person of the most serious criminal charges. This result is almost as bad as a complete acquittal. There are a few instances where the state is lucky enough to have a complete, air-tight case. In these cases, there is little doubt of the defendant's guilt, thereby giving the defense little or no wiggle room. When this occurs, the defense will usually try and negotiate a plea. If the case goes to trial they will contend that their client is crazy, and therefore was not responsible for his/her actions. They then will hire their hired gun psychiatrist to testify their examination proved the individual was nuts at the time he committed the crime. At the same time, the state has their psychiatrist testify that the defendant was sane and responsible for his/her actions. The defense usually uses this 'insane' approach as a last resort since history shows that it is usually not very successful.

The trial date was creeping closer every day, and Sullivan was not at all happy with the status of his investigation. It seemed everything he followed up on either turned out to be a dead end or could not be substantiated. Sullivan heard a rumor that an individual named Al Charles was running his mouth around town. Apparently, Charles knew what happened concerning the murder and was directly involved. Sullivan was familiar with Charles, and knew there was little chance that he really had anything to do with the crime. He was most likely just looking for attention, a free drink, or a hit of whatever drug was around. He was known as "Crazy Al" because of his antics and wild tales, especially when he was out of his mind on drugs and/or booze.

Experience taught Sullivan that he had to practice "defensive police work" in order to give defense attorneys less fodder to criticize the investigator with at the trial. If this lead had not been followed up on and Bridgeport's attorneys heard about Al Charles, they would, of course, say *he* was the real killer. If only the incompetent, negligent, and lazy investigator had followed up and pursued Al Charles, he would have the *real* killer on trial instead of their poor, innocent, and framed client, Mr. Bridgeport!

Sullivan looked up Al Charles and easily found him in his trailer that he rented in a rundown trailer park (Is there any other kind?). Sullivan knocked on the rickety door several times and finally Charles responded. *I'm coming. Hold your goddamn horses!* Sullivan heard from inside.

It was approaching noon, but Al Charles had not gotten out of bed as of yet. He opened the door wearing only a pair of filthy-looking boxer shorts. The stench from inside the trailer hit Sullivan in the face like a ton of bricks. That was one thing about Sullivan's job…he dealt with human debris, scum, and the trash of life. He was left no choice but to get right in there and rub elbows with them. Many times, Sullivan felt like he needed to be deloused and soaked in a steaming hot shower, which is what he usually did. But hey, no complaints came out of Sullivan's mouth. After all, a police officer's pay in 1980 made it all worthwhile…right?

Charles looked surprised to see what was standing on his stoop. Sullivan, seeing that look before, asked to step in and talk to him for a few minutes. Al opened the door wider, signaling for Sullivan to come in.

"What the fuck do you want with me? I ain't raped or killed nobody," Charles pleaded.

Sullivan knew he was wasting his time having to talk to an idiot like this, but felt it needed to be covered regardless. Sullivan walked into the living room and sat down on a stained and torn couch.

"Al, what do you know about the Beth Cowens murder?" Sullivan questioned.

"Are you shittin' me? I don't know a God dammed thing about that, nor do I want to know anything!"

"That's not what I hear. From my understanding, you've been shooting your mouth off about participating in the murder!"

"Aw hell, Sullivan, you know how I am when I'm drunk or high. Shit, I'm liable to say anything about anything! But, I sure as hell don't know anything about that. I didn't even know the Cowens girl. The only thing I know about Tater Bridgeport is the dope I've bought from him…pretty shitty stuff."

Sullivan knew Al was telling the truth. He was not really capable of being involved in something like this. If Charles' brain was cotton, the combination of alcohol, drugs, and inbreeding left it the inability to be even a Kotex for a mosquito. Sullivan asked Al what he knew about Harry Seasons. He said he got wasted with Seasons a few times. Charles also mentioned Seasons would stick his dick in a snake's mouth if someone would be willing to hold its head. Sullivan laughed then asked Charles to keep his ears to the ground. If he heard anything reliable about the murder, let Sullivan know and he would make it worth his while if the information panned out.

Sullivan kept hearing rumors of a big drug/orgy type of party that got out of hand the night Beth was killed. However, the scene did not show any signs of a large number of people at the murder scene, unless the party was held somewhere else. Beth would have been brought to the rural area of the cornfield in order to dump the body to give the false impression that the murder happened there. Sullivan questioned every doper, tramp, criminal, and jail-inmate in Poland County, but could not find any substantiation for the drug/orgy party that allegedly took place on that night. Was Sullivan chasing his own tail?

CHAPTER THIRTEEN - AN OVERWEIGHT WOMAN LACKING A FEW, SORELY-NEEDED TEETH

The trial date was approaching fast. Sullivan had to face the fact that he was going to trial with the evidence he had and hope for the best. In a last desperate attempt to get more information on Harry Seasons's possible involvement in the murder, Sullivan decided to contact the underbelly of Poland County to see if they could get Harry Seasons to talk about or hopefully admit to the murder of Beth Cowens. If they were willing to get information from Harry Seasons as Sullivan asked them to, Sullivan knew they could not testify as to what Seasons had told them because they were acting as informants of Detective Sullivan. However, if Sullivan could independently substantiate any of the information, it could be used against Seasons.

The two individuals Sullivan felt he had the best chance of getting something out of Seasons were Joe Rogers and Billy Most. Sullivan helped them in the past, and he knew they were in the drug scene. Helping matters, they ran with the same crowd as Harry Seasons. Sullivan contacted Rogers first and convinced him to see what he could find out. Although it was not ethical, he gave Rogers money for expenses to "party" with Seasons. Sullivan then contacted Billy Most and did the same thing with him. Sullivan believed it was desperation time. He had to get all the information he could in one, final desperate attempt. Then, he would follow up on the information, in hopes it would lead to not only evidence against Harry Seasons, but possibly additional evidence against Larry 'Tater' Bridgeport. Sullivan gave Rogers and Most several weeks to get something out of Seasons. He first contacted Rogers to see if he received anything incriminating.

"Man I tried! I partied with Seasons three or four times, got him high as a kite, but couldn't get him to admit to anything. All he would talk about was that you were on his case. He told me you wanted him to take a lie detector test. He was afraid to because he thought you were trying to frame him with the results. I pressed him and told him he could tell me; that I wouldn't say anything to anybody, but I couldn't get him to admit to anything. I really don't think he had anything to do with it. If he did, he's sure scared to talk about it! He said you told him you were gonna get him and put him in the gas chamber for something he had nothing to do with," Rogers explained.

Rogers seemed like he had really tried to get information out of Seasons, but just could not get the job done. Sullivan then contacted Most to see if he did any better than Rogers. Unfortunately, Sullivan received just about the same story verbatim from Most that he had from Rogers. Sullivan was pissed that his money and time were completely wasted since nothing came of their partying together. Sullivan knew it was time to meet with the prosecutor and start making preparations for the trial against Bridgeport. It was now time to "fish or cut bait" as the old saying went.

Although the prosecutor already had the autopsy report from the forensic pathologist, Archer still wanted to sit down with the pathologist and go over his examination and accompanying photographs. The conversation was mostly of a technical and medical nature, with the pathologist going over each photograph and explaining the relevant injuries, and the ultimate consequences of each one. While listening to the forensic pathologist describe Beth's body as if it were a piece of equipment that had been fatally damaged, Sullivan could not help but think of what Beth must have gone through—the physical pain, the fear, the disbelief of what was actually happening to her, and trying desperately to think of some way to escape the overwhelming situation. Her attempt to save her life by running away obviously was a complete and utter failure. This resulted in…

1) Her being shot numerous times.
2) Her back carved on like an ancient ritual.
3) Something the size of a baseball bat rammed up her rectum.
4) Her being run over by a vehicle, resulting in the obliteration of her face.

According to the pathologist, most or all of this occurred while Beth was still alive and most likely conscious. Even though Sullivan often observed man's inhumanity to man (in this case woman), this was the most extreme case he had ever observed or experienced. To say he was disgusted was an understatement.

Events in Sullivan's life, this case in particular, were really affecting him personally. When he was not working, he spent most of his time in his favorite hangout, the Bobtail Inn. His home life was almost non-existent. Other than being around his children, he really could have cared less if he ever went home or not. The pressure of this case was increasing every day as the trial date got closer and closer. Sullivan's nerves were about shot, so he dealt with it all by drinking way more than he should have. Sullivan's supervisor, Detective-In-Charge Knapp, found out about Sullivan's activities by means Sullivan was unaware of. Making his day, Sullivan was contacted by his favorite and knowledgeable supervisor in reference to his alcohol intake.

"I understand you've been doing a lot of drinking," Knapp stated.

"Yeah, what's it to you?" Sullivan wondered.

"Well, some of it has been in the afternoon before you're even off duty! This has to stop immediately or I'll see to it you're out of a job," Knapp threatened.

Sullivan, with his nerves already frayed to the limit, responded, "You son-of-a-bitch! I've forgotten more about this job than you'll ever know! You don't know your ass from a hole in the ground when it comes to real police work...and to think you're going to get my job? Hell, you wouldn't even have this supervisor's job if the First Sergeant could've gotten you to do anything out in the field! He told me himself the only reason he made you DIC was because he couldn't get you to do what you were supposed to! At least this way he could have you in here checking reports. If you want a piece of my ass you don't have to get it this way. Let's just go out back and settle it like men!"

By this time Sullivan's voice had risen to a high pitch. He knew Knapp could have filed departmental insubordination charges against him, but he really was not concerned about that. He was venting and nothing or no one was going to shut him up. Sullivan finally concluded what he had to say.

"If a sorry, sack-of-shit like you can get my job, it's not worth having anyway. Do whatever you want!"

Sullivan *stormed* out of Knapp's office disgusted and indignant. *How dare that incompetent prick speak to him in that manner?* He decided to hit the Bobtail Inn and really tear one on. *No son-of-a-bitch was going to tell me what to do*, he thought to himself. *Hell, I've put more criminals in jail by accident than Knapp ever did on purpose and everybody knows it, including Knapp himself.* Knapp already informed Sullivan he was going to call him out on every homicide investigation in the district because of his track record of solving them and his experience. In Sullivan's career he had solved every homicide he had been in charge of except one. That case in particular actually occurred in Illinois. The body just happened to float to the Indiana side of the river. He was convinced he found out who committed that murder. He just could not prove it. That was how things went sometimes.

After getting warmed up at the Bobtail Inn, Harry decided to head to Morganville to patronize the Victory Lounge, one of the oldest bars around in the area. At this fine establishment, they used to have go-go girls dancing on the weekends. Now, the only dancing done was by the partiers. The music played used to vary, depending on the night of the week. Now, it was mostly disco-type songs. Harry liked the Victory Lounge better the way it was in the late sixties. The cigarette smoke in the air was enough to choke the average person. That didn't change.

Harry walked in, almost coughed, and surveyed the scene. Several women and a few men were on the dance floor, moving to "Upside Down" by

Diana Ross. He leisurely walked up to the bar and ordered a 7 and 7. After paying the bartender, Harry sat down next to a female who had dirty blond hair and what appeared to be a decent set of knockers. He surmised that she was probably in her early-to-mid forties, a tad older than Harry. He also noticed that her well-rounded ass covered the entire bar stool, with a little hanging over both sides (actually a lot). With the success Harry usually had with women, he figured this was probably about as good as he was going to get on this or any night. Like a heathen, he thought to himself, *Hell, if I buy her a few drinks, maybe I'll get lucky.* Believe it or not, Harry felt guilty about doing this—possibly cheating on his wife. However, he knew if he went home and got into bed, it would be the same old, worn-out story.

I'm tired.

Leave me alone.

Most likely due to the recent stress of his work and home life, Harry was just not in the mood for that on this particular evening. He needed someone to talk to at the very least. If that individual pretended like they were attracted to him that would be a bonus. *Lie to me, if you have to*, Harry thought. With the alcohol starting to take over, Harry asked the pudgy dishwater-blond setting on the stool next to him if he could buy her a drink. She had what appeared to be an unfiltered cigarette sticking out of the corner of her mouth. Harry was not sure if that was a turn-on or not.

"I guess," she replied.

Knowing he was likely looking for love in all the wrong places, Harry removed his wedding ring prior to entering. Harry could not help but notice the strong odor of cheap perfume all over the woman. It went pretty well with the equally cheap cologne that radiated off him. When she spoke, Harry noticed her teeth obviously had some problems, like one or two missing. Harry already had several drinks at the Bobtail Inn and the lights were low, keeping visuals a bit fuzzy. With those variables in play, she appeared to be a pretty good catch for the evening. Harry knew he was no Ricardo Montalban or Fernando Llamas, so why be so picky?

Suddenly, a slow song started playing, "All Out of Love" by Air Supply. It was not Harry's type of music, but it was popular at the time. Regardless of his personal preference, the song *was* a slow one so Harry asked the woman if she would like to dance. She responded again with the same ecstatic answer she gave when he offered to buy her a drink.

"I guess."

As they began to bump and grind a little, he told her his real name. He could have given her a fake name, but why bother? She said her name was Margaret. It was not the sexiest name ever, but it would do for this evening.

As Harry held her close and danced to the limp and wimpy tune, he complimented her dancing skills. Buttering her up even more, Harry told her how attractive she was and how fantastic she smelled. Harry was lying through his teeth, of course, but there was a method to his madness.

After finishing the dance, Harry and Margaret went back over to the bar and continued drinking their respective drinks. Harry knew he would have to tell her what he did for a living if he was lucky (or unlucky) enough to get laid. Even though his car was unmarked, it was obviously a police car of some kind, with the radios and such. Harry was too cheap to spring even for a dingy motel room, so they would have to do the dirty deed in the backseat of his vehicle…either that or in an alley (just kidding).

After several more drinks and dances, Harry asked Margaret if she was hungry and had a way home. She responded she did not have a way home, and was hungry. With that, out the door of the smoke-filled lounge they went.

They got into Harry's police car that sat in the dimly-lit parking lot. The time for talk was over. The time for action had begun. After a few minutes, it became all too clear that this was not Margaret's first rodeo. Harry wondered to himself how many guys had 'parked' with Margaret before this night? He feared what that number might be.

It had been a month since Harry had been intimate, so it did not take long at all for the act to be over with. Once they were finished, they cuddled (if you want to call it that) for awhile. Margaret told him what a good lover he was. Harry knew that was a lie. No other woman on his short list of lovers ever told him that before. Harry knew Margaret just trying to be nice, so he returned the compliment. Harry was not necessarily lying on this one. It *was* the best sex he had in a few years.

Harry bummed a cigarette from Margaret and lit hers as well. He was always trying to quit and, therefore, rarely had any smokes on him. He and Margaret talked for several more minutes. After ignoring his rumbling stomach and noticing it was around three in the morning, Harry decided to get something to eat. He and his newfound companion drove to an all-night, greasy-spoon diner. To Harry, taking her to this establishment was a thoughtful and romantic gesture; a way of saying, *Thank you for sleeping with me on the first night you met me.*

By this time it was about daylight, so Harry took Margaret to her apartment located on Edgar Street, in the inner city of Morganville. She gave Harry a quick kiss and asked if they could see one another again. Harry said he would call her, but never bothered to ask for her phone number or last name. That pretty much confirmed that this relationship was a one night stand—something Harry was very seldom able to make happen. Many of his colleagues got more ass than a toilet seat, and that did not even include their wives. However, getting some strange was pretty much foreign to Harry. On the rare occasion he managed to give a woman a later regret, he always felt guilty afterwards. Harry's marriage was lousy. His wife did not give a damn about him. However, he *was* married. In addition to that, she did give birth to the children he adored more than anything. Harry felt he was stuck between a rock and a hard place. Margaret walked towards her front door, with her behind looking like two giant water balloons stuffed into some denim.

CHAPTER FOURTEEN - A DEPRESSED AND WORRIED MAN

The trial, which had been moved to Harrison County due to prejudicial publicity, was only a couple of weeks away. Sullivan and the prosecutor already met with the pathologist in regards to his testimony. They were now getting ready to prepare their witness list. Sullivan, who was the chief witness, had the most damaging testimony against Bridgeport. Other than testimony from police-related witnesses, the other important witnesses were Joe Broshears and Linda Selbey.

They were the witnesses who could put Bridgeport and Beth Cowens together the very night she was murdered. Sullivan kept in touch with them every week or two in order to make sure they had not changed the important eyewitness information they previously offered. Sullivan found nothing to question his belief that Broshears and Selbey were telling the truth and were keeping to their stories.

Sullivan received a troubling phone call that, if experience was any indication, could absolutely derail the case against Bridgeport. The call was from DEA agent Dale Cunningham. Sullivan was not very familiar with him, but had met him on a few occasions. For a Fed, he seemed like a pretty up-front type of guy. Cunningham opened the conversation with some small talk, and then got to his point.

"The federal prosecutor is going to be in my office Monday morning. I was wondering if you and the local prosecutor could meet with us? It's important."

"I don't know. I think I can make it, but I can't speak for Archer. If you can tell me what the meeting is about, I'll run it by him," Sullivan responded.

"It's regarding the status of Mr. Bridgeport. He has been doing some very important work for the federal government, and we want to discuss it with you and the local prosecutor," Cunningham answered.

Sullivan had been through this kind of situation before where a defendant is an informant for the Feds and they want some cooperation from the local police and prosecutor so their golden goose can continue laying eggs. In most cases, the state had to yield to the federal government's wishes. However, this was different because Bridgeport was charged with a particularly heinous crime.

"I'll run it by the prosecutor and let you know if he can meet with you. However, he is extremely busy right now preparing for this murder trial, so if he has time, you may have to meet us in his office. Plus, to be honest with you, I don't think he will be in the mood to do any favors for Bridgeport because of the seriousness of the charges against him," Sullivan informed Cunningham.

With that, the conversation ended. Sullivan proceeded to the prosecutor's office to inform him of his conversation with Cunningham. Archer was immediately livid.

"If those assholes think for one minute I'm going to help them at the cost of helping Bridgeport so their asses are covered on little drug cases, they're crazy! You tell them I will extend the courtesy to speak with them in *my* office at *my* convenience. However, make it clear to them we're not making any deals. For Christ's sake, the son-of-a-bitch committed the most gruesome murder in our county's history! He's damn lucky we're not seeking the death penalty. If it wasn't for the fact that seeking the death penalty would make a conviction a lot tougher and would at the same time, nearly bankrupt the county, I'd be seeking it!" Archer eloquently explained.

Sullivan assured him he would relay the message to Cunningham. Sullivan decided not to break tradition, so he headed to his local watering hole again after work. Harry sat down, ordered a cold beer and depressingly thought to himself, *What a fucking life. I can't go home, nor do I want to. I have a job that doesn't pay worth a damn. If this murder trial goes down the toilet, I'll get all of the blame for sure!*

The beers went down smooth as they always did. After several, Harry relaxed enough to begin enjoying himself as much as was possible considering his state of mind. A pair of good-looking women walked in the door and sat down at the bar. Harry was not familiar with these two, but thought he would try and start a conversation with them. It was probably a long shot because even the lesser of the two appeared to be *way* too attractive for him.

"Girls, my name is Harry Sullivan. May I buy you fine-looking ladies a drink?"

They both looked at Sullivan and said in unison, almost as if it had been rehearsed, "No thanks, we're waiting for someone."

It would have hurt his pride, but Harry did not have any pride left to hurt. Maybe a heavyset girl might walk in at any moment. That was more his type anyway—the type who does not have much going on in any department whatsoever.

The meeting was quickly set up in Archer's office with the Feds. They were, of course, so nice that sugar would not melt in their mouths. The talk was of cooperation, the "big picture", etc., etc. They finally got to the point and spoke of candor and confidentiality.

"Look, Bridgeport has been working with us for a year or so, and his testimony can put several of the biggest suppliers of controlled substances in federal prison for years. The suppliers are from the El Paso area. They supply the entire Midwest, including Southern Indiana," one DEA agent explained.

"Bridgeport insists he didn't kill the girl. He confessed to allowing the guys from El Paso borrow his truck and Beth Cowens on the night of the murder. They were up making a delivery to him. Bridgeport said things were getting heated for various reasons, and to cool things off, he let them borrow both as an olive branch. Now, he feels he's being set up to take the fall for the El Paso dealers," the second DEA agent said.

"We need him to be released for a little while longer to get a few more bits of information and evidence so this whole year won't be for nothing," the first DEA agent requested.

"This is horseshit! We've got plenty of evidence to place him at the scene. He had motive, opportunity, and a hundred other things pointing to him as committing this murder. Besides, we can't release him back on the street. He'll flee! He killed someone, for Christ's sake!" Sullivan yelled.

"Look, you guys are famous for wiretaps and things like that. Do you have proof of any kind that these so-called drug kings from Texas have anything to do with the murder of Beth Cowens?" asked Archer.

Their answer was 'no,' which pretty much ended the conversation and the meeting. Without the stamp-of-approval from the local prosecutor and lead detective, it would be difficult to force the release of a murder suspect, especially considering the evidence. Nothing more was heard from the Feds after this meeting, but Sullivan could not help but wonder if Bridgeport's attorney might use this ploy to allege that Bridgeport was framed and had nothing to do with the crime. It seemed awfully farfetched, but Sullivan had seen weirder things tried by defense attorneys in his career.

Even though Sullivan knew any truth to the tale about a Texas drug cartel framing Bridgeport was as likely as a snowball's chance in Hell, he knew it would be wise for him to check the story out as much as possible. Sullivan did not have it as easy as a defense attorney did. A defense lawyer did not have to substantiate anything. All he/she had to do was raise a possible scenario of how an allegation or suggestion might explain away a fact or a set of facts. That would hopefully put doubt in the jury's mind for them to come up with a 'not guilty' verdict, or at least guilt of a lesser offense.

Unfortunately, Sullivan knew he was not going to get any help or information out of the Feds. So he thought he might contact the state police narcotics section and the Morganville narcotics unit to see if they knew anything about Bridgeport and this supposed conspiracy to set him up as the fall guy.

    Sullivan contacted ISP narcotics officer, Norman Hechelmeister, who was a friend of his, and sort-of a legend in his own right. He was so good at what he did, and was so respected by other law enforcement agencies, that the Feds frequently recruited him to work for them in Mississippi, Texas, Florida, California, and Arizona. He had been with the state police narcotics section since its inception.

    Sullivan explained to Hechelmeister the story of what the Feds relayed to him. Hechelmeister responded he knew nothing of it. Sullivan was not surprised. Hechelmeister explained he was recently in California, working for the FBI on a federal task force concerning drugs that were originating out of Northern California. Most of the illegal drugs from there ended up in the Chicago, Gary, and Hammond areas. Hechelmeister mentioned he did hear about the Cowens murder, but knew nothing regarding the outlandish information that Bridgeport supposedly provided the DEA. He did say he would see what he could find out concerning the information provided by the Feds, and would let Sullivan know if he learned anything.

    Sullivan strongly believed Harry Seasons was involved in the murder. If his reputation held true, Seasons probably had more to do with the murder (especially the sexual assault) than Bridgeport did. The only problem was that Sullivan could not prove it. In Sullivan' mind, only three people knew for sure what happened that fateful night—Bridgeport, Seasons, and Beth Cowens. Bridgeport lawyered up and was not talking. Seasons would not admit to anything. Beth was dead, so she certainly could not provide any information to Sullivan. Although it was complete fantasy, Sullivan often thought about how helpful it would have been if the dead could somehow come back and explain actually what happened and who the perpetrator(s) were. If that were possible, however, Harry most likely would have been back writing traffic tickets for a living.

    Harry's home life was, as usual, just about intolerable. Harry knew part of the problem was due to the circumstances surrounding his job. The amount of pressure he felt for solving murders, robberies, assaults, and rapes was unbelievable. Victims and/or their families counted on Harry to find the person or persons responsible and put them behind bars to give them satisfaction and closure. That was one of the many reasons why he drank so much and so often.

    His wife appeared to be satisfied as long as she could continue living in her own little world. Belinda did only the bare basics, especially when it came to taking care of her children and her husband. At this stage of the marriage, she had absolutely nothing in common with Harry. Worse yet, she did what a lot of middle-aged women do when they reach their mid-thirties. Belinda completely let herself go—she gained weight, cut off her previously long, beautiful hair, and painted her face with makeup until she looked almost like a clown. Belinda endured sex with Harry infrequently, with as little enthusiasm as possible.

Harry often reflected back to the time when he was a reasonably young trooper. One time, he was involved in a fatal traffic accident while en route to an accident. His lights and siren were on, but that did not stop an old woman from pulling out right in front of Harry, making it almost impossible to avoid ramming into her vehicle. The police cruiser burst into flames with Harry trapped inside the car. He barely managed to escape the burning vehicle with his life. When another officer took him home after the accident, looking like the walking dead, Belinda looked him up and down and did not even bother asking what happened. Needless to say, she did not shed a tear later on when Harry finally informed her of how close he came to death.

That incident should have raised a huge red flag, but as stated earlier, Harry never had much luck when it came to the fairer sex. He certainly was not the strongest wolf among the pack when it came to romanticizing women. In some ways, Harry felt he should be fairly appreciative that *someone* chose to spend their life with him.

Harry recalled occasions when he was having sex with Belinda. He honestly thought he was doing a good job, humping away and touching her in all the right places. It was then that he would be interrupted by the sound of Belinda laughing at something on television, or her yawning, indicating a sheer sense of boredom.

I love you? Forget about it. Those words were seldom, if ever, said to one another. There was just no passion, interest, or desire whatsoever in the relationship. Where was the woman he married? She was pretty then. They had fun together and seemed to have things in common. Was it Harry who was the one who had changed? He did not think that was the problem. He was pretty much the same ornery guy he was when he met her. Could it have been the job? If anything, he was able to be home more now versus when he was a trooper, working the highways. It all just dumbfounded Harry how everything went from good to bad in a matter of just a few years. Unfortunately, the ones who suffered the most in this situation were Harry's children—the two people he wanted the least to be affected by this mess of a marriage. They were the only ones who kept Harry from leaving Belinda.

Just when Harry was at his lowest point, he began speaking with a woman in his neighborhood who seemed to revitalize him. The conversation started after they saw each other around town several times. It did not take long at all for both to realize they lived in the same neighborhood. She was quite attractive and as nice as anyone Harry had met in a long time. What puzzled Harry was that she actually seemed to enjoy Sullivan's company and showed a real interest in him and his work.

She was married to a local businessman who did not mistreat her or their children in any way. All in all, it sounded like he was a pretty good guy. The only problem seemed to be a lack of time management. Apparently, he had very little time for her or the children between his job and his hobby of playing golf. She was a true golf widow when he was not working twelve hours a day. She was married to a true-blue 'work-golfaholic.' She did not know Belinda, but no one in the neighborhood really did. Belinda stayed indoors most of the time and rarely socialized with the neighbors. This newfound friend of Harry's did know his children though. Her kids began frequently playing with his. Speaking about the kids became a regular topic of conversation.

Their interest in each other started innocently enough, however it quickly escalated into a much more intimate and personal relationship. The woman's name was Diana Kleemer. Harry could not imagine why a woman who was as pretty as she was would want to have anything to do with a loser like him. It was ironic her name was Diana because many people, including Harry, said she resembled Princess Diana.

Confusing Harry even more, she genuinely seemed to worry about Harry. Diana knew his job was dangerous. Sometimes, when Harry did not get home when she thought he should have, Diana would call his residence when she observed him pulling into the driveway. Harry's home was in view from her house. By the sound of it, her late nights were not filled with reasons keeping her in the bedroom. The calls were usually late at night or very early in the morning by the time Harry got home, but that did not seem to matter to Diana. She checked on him often to make sure he was alright. Harry was touched by the gestures. Belinda was always fast asleep when he got home, in order to be well-rested for church, to visit her family, or for shopping. Sullivan never asked Diana to go out, mainly because he got to know her husband and children. He was not trying to be a home wrecker. He might have been willing to have a one night stand with a woman who had teeth like a jack-o-lantern, but he didn't want to break up a family. One evening though, Harry got home at a reasonable hour for a change. The phone began ringing.

"Hey, this is Diana. What's going on?"

"Oh, just tired and worried about this upcoming trial. If that bastard gets off, I'll have to leave the county!"

"If you do, can you take me with you?" Diana wondered.

Both laughed.

"I don't know if you have figured it out yet, but I'm kind of crazy about you," Diana confessed.

This shocked Harry to say the least.

"What have you been drinking tonight? Whatever it is, I'll have some of it!" Harry retorted.

Again, both laughed.

"You don't really mean that. Hell, you have a good husband and three beautiful kids. Besides, who in their right mind would want someone like me?" Harry wondered.

"We have talked for long time now. I can't really explain it, but I have never felt this way about anyone like I do you. All I know is I want to be with you and I think about you constantly."

"Look Diana, you're just going through something right now. I am flattered that someone as beautiful and as nice as you would even give me the time of day. Please believe that! However, I would never want to break up your home and end up hurting your children, not to mention your husband."

Harry's words seemed to snap her back into reality. They spoke for a minute or two more and then the conversation was over, as were their illusions of being together. They both knew their situations were too involved and complicated to really go there. Harry wondered why he could not have met her twenty years ago? Such is life.

Speaking of life, Harry's upbringing was pretty typical of a kid born in the mid-1940's. Harry grew up in a small, rural town about 100 miles from Poland County. He had a brother, Earl Sullivan, Jr., who was a few years older than Harry. His parents were essentially typical products of the depression— either worried about every dime, or spending everything they got their hands on. In their particular case, it was the former. They held on to every penny they got with a death grip. People from that generation *never* bought anything they wanted, even if you could afford it. They only bought what they needed.

Harry's father, a man he greatly admired and loved, worried about anything and everything. Earl, Sr. was an independent cattle trader. He would purchase cattle from local farmers. The routine would be Earl, Sr. looking at what was available, guessing the cattle's weight and quality, and if an agreeable price could be reached, would usually purchase several head of them. He would then take them to market, usually at a few select, small packing houses. Harry could remember his father 'dickering' with the buyer about how much the cattle were worth per pound.

"Goddamn it, I can't even make a haul bill out of what you're offering me! Hell, you know these cattle are worth more than that," Earl, Sr.

protested.

After finally settling on a price, Earl, Sr. would leave, complaining all the way home. With a burning Lucky Strike hanging out of his mouth, Earl, Sr. would let Harry know more than he probably should have.

"Hell, you can't make a Goddamn living at this cattle trading anymore! These sons-a-bitches want to steal them from you," Earl, Sr. exclaimed.

Harry recalled plenty of times at the dinner table (*promptly* at 6pm, especially in the summer time), setting down to a big, unhealthy meal consisting of fried chicken or pork shoulder with fried potatoes and milk gravy, all cooked in *lard*. Almost every dinner consisted of the same conversation.

"I don't know what I'm going to do. This cattle trading has gone to hell!" Earl, Sr. complained.

As a kid, Harry got to the point where he was worried about having enough money to pay the bills, his dad being able to keep a roof over their heads, and food in their bellies. It never got to that point, but his dad had him convinced that it was right around the corner.

Harry's mother was one of a kind; maybe not back then, but definitely in today's world. Like her husband, Naomi Sullivan watched *every dime*. However, while Earl, Sr. was the provider, Naomi took care of the home. She was very much the motherly type. Harry never had to make his bed or fix his own lunch. He was probably five years-old before he started wiping his own ass! Naomi was always there to wait on him and his brother hand and foot. That was just the way she and most mothers in the 1950's did things.

Harry's older brother was the intelligent one with the good looks. Harry often thought he must have been adopted or secretly dropped off on the door step of his parents' home by some poor, uneducated girl who just happened to get knocked up by some idiot. Harry could never figure out why school was so easy for Earl, Jr. and so difficult for Harry? If they came from the same two people, then why was Earl, Jr. so handsome and Harry was so…not?

Harry obviously had issues from childbirth that added to his current dilemma. The end result of both was a depressed and worried man, who drank his troubles away. Could this troubled man handle this murder investigation to its conclusion? Only time would tell.

CHAPTER FIFTEEN - THE TRIAL (PART I)

It was finally time for the trial to begin. Sullivan did everything he knew to do in order to get a conviction. He had been through big trials before, but none as important as this one. This was the most gruesome and horrific murder that had ever been committed in Poland County (possibly in the entire state of Indiana). Anything short of a first-degree murder conviction would be considered a complete and utter failure. Sullivan knew this and felt every ounce of the pressure. He was the one who arrested Bridgeport and accused him of this crime. A finding of innocence or conviction of a lesser charge would not only reflect badly on Sullivan, but on the state police as well.

Juries are made up of people, and people always bothered Sullivan. Regardless of the facts, they could be swayed. He could never tell what they were thinking. The average person has no idea of the people in society that are just downright cruel with no conscious. They are capable of doing the unspeakable to anyone for absolutely no reason. The nature of human beings is to try and see the good in people. They do not want to believe or see the worst in defendants. When someone pleads 'not guilty,' the majority of people of the jury want to believe them.

"Intellectual idiots," as Sullivan called them, were intellectuals in the field of criminal behavior. They did not believe anyone was truly mean or evil. They believed the defendants were sick, and gave those individuals names like "paranoid." To Sullivan, who had to deal with their handiwork, it really did not matter what label was put on them. In his experience and opinion, those individuals could never be cured or rehabilitated. For the protection of the rest of society, they had to be eliminated by execution, or at the very least incarcerated for life.

It was now officially ShowTime. Sullivan was going to find out if his hard work was going to pay off or not. Archer and Sullivan spent several weeks preparing their case by organizing evidence, witnesses, and strategy. The first order of official trial business would be the selection of a jury.

The legal term for this act of futility was "void ire." It involved the court notifying a number of citizens of the county the trial was going to be held in, to be at the courthouse at a certain date and time for the jury selection process. The citizens who were contacted to be available for jury service were given a form to fill out with several questions concerning their names, addresses, ages, and other pertinent information concerning themselves. This information, along with the questioning of the prospective jurors, would hopefully assist the defense and prosecution to find as impartial a jury as was possible. However, this really was not what either side wanted.

The defense wanted someone who would naturally lean toward them, concerning their attitudes and thoughts. Likewise, the prosecution wanted jurors who would lean toward the prosecution's point of view. Some considered the picking of a favorable jury sort of a science in itself, but Sullivan's experience indicated it was nothing more than a roll of the dice. The following were indicators used in questioning prospective jurors:

1) Did he/she have any relatives or close friends in law enforcement?
2) Did he/she have any previous arrests or run-ins with the police?
3) Did he/she have any knowledge of the defendant or prospective witnesses?
4) If he/she felt the defendant was guilty of the crime charged beyond a reasonable doubt, could they vote to convict him and send him to prison for the rest of his life without the possibility of parole?

These and other similar considerations were things that the defense and prosecution tried to determine in picking an impartial jury, if there was such a thing.

The first day of the trial Bridgeport looked more like a kid showing up for his first day of school than he did a defendant in a gruesome murder trial. He was clean shaven with a fresh haircut. His handlers put Bridgeport into a new suit. He certainly did not look like a torturer and murderer, at least not on this particular morning.

The Harrison Circuit Court Judge entered the courtroom and proceeded to his throne. He proceeded to say a few words advising everyone of what they were there for, as if they were a bunch of idiots. The ceremony (circus) was officially underway.

The judge proceeded to call the first twelve citizens who were there to do their official duty as potential jurors. If they were not selected, they would go back to their worlds of life and luxury. The questioning of each prospective juror began in earnest by the prosecution and defense, trying to determine any knowledge, prejudices, or pre-conceived notions about this case. The objective of the whole procedure was, of course, to find an impartial group of people to hear the evidence that was to be presented, and make a determination of guilt or innocence based solely on the evidence presented. It sounded good in theory, but true justice, even if everything went according to an executed plan, was seldom, if ever, reached. Sullivan believed that only God held true justice in His hands, and He was the only entity who could dispense it. Man's feeble attempts usually came up horribly short under the best of circumstances.

Sullivan really did not believe the case would take over a week to fully complete. In his mind, it was open and shut. As it turned out though, jury selection took two days by itself. The trial then began with opening arguments by the prosecution in reference to what they intended to prove beyond a reasonable doubt. The defense stated their theory of the case, particularly the presumption of innocence of their "framed" client, whom they reiterated the jury should have sympathy for because he had been falsely accused. Because of the incompetence and almost criminal negligence of the state and their chief investigator, Detective Harold Sullivan, Mr. Bridgeport had been falsely accused from the get-go of this horrific crime. In turn, the real murderer or murderers were running the streets, eager to rape and kill again!

The state's first witness was the owner of the farm ground and the man who discovered Beth Cowens's nude, dead body lying in his cornfield. He gave his account of checking his crops just after dawn on the early morning in question. He told how he noticed the corn stalks in his field had been knocked down in a "horseshoe" fashion by what he felt was some kind of a vehicle. Upon further inspection, he said he observed something lying among the corn stalks that had been flattened. At first, he believed it to be a dead animal, perhaps a deer. As he approached the carcass, he quickly realized it was the body of a human being.

The next witnesses were the two deputy sheriffs who responded to the scene after law enforcement was contacted. Their testimony was short, only concerning arriving at the scene, observing the body, and securing the scene until Detective Sullivan arrived to take over.

The chief witness, Harold Sullivan, was then called to the witness box. His testimony went smoothly during the state's portion of the questioning. After the routine preliminary questions were asked by the prosecutor, the testimony began in earnest reference Sullivan's actions on that fateful day.

Sullivan testified to exactly what he observed upon arriving at the scene. He said the first thing he did was to make sure the scene was protected and preserved. He then removed everyone from the scene except police and police-related personnel. He notified the state police post to send necessary investigative and crime scene technician officers to the scene. He then interviewed the owner of the farm ground who discovered the body. After Joe Rallings arrived on the scene, along with a couple of other state police officers, the on-scene evidentiary and photography investigation ensued. All items of evidence were carefully located, examined, photographed and recovered from the scene. Sullivan testified as to the description of the female body lying bloody, bruised, and lifeless among the flattened corn stalks. His testimony continued in regards to his observations concerning the murder scene, and what he and other officers did and did not do concerning their on the scene investigation. This took an entire day to complete.

The next day's testimony covered the detective part of the investigation. Sullivan spoke about discovering the chrome strip that had light green paint residue on it, paint chips, corn stalks sticking out of the undercarriage, shell casings located in the bed of the truck, and a broken necklace found in the cab. He then testified to his initial, futile attempts to get the murder victim identified.

The defense had not objected much concerning Sullivan's testimony up to this point. However, when he started testifying directly about their client, the defense suddenly came to life and began objecting to the court concerning almost every question Sullivan was asked and every answer he provided. Most of the objections were for minor legal points like "leading questions," the "relevance" of the questions, etc. The judge ruled in favor of the state on most objections, and seemed to finally get irritated with the defense. The judge finally scolded the defense attorneys and things seemed to go smoother after that.

No one really knew what time Bridgeport arrived home, except for his mother. Sullivan covered that base early on by interviewing her before she spoke to Bridgeport to discuss the situation and get their stories/timetables to coincide. When Sullivan testified to this, the defense, of course, strongly objected. They knew this would be a problem. The defense team would probably try to explain it away by calling Bridgeport's mother to the stand to testify that she was confused and intimidated when she spoke to the detective that morning. Naturally, what she told him was a mistake or he misconstrued what she said. Next up was the defense's turn giving Sullivan the Spanish Inquisition.

The biggest three-word phrase in a defense attorney's lexicon is, *is it possible?* They love to use this phrase as often as they can, in hopes that the uneducated and mal-informed jurors will substitute the word "possible" for the word "probable." Sullivan's experience was that this was how lawyers, doctors, and other intellectual types look at the average person that usually makes up a jury. After all, a defense attorney's job is not to uncover the truth. Instead, it is to raise doubt about prosecution's case that tends to show the guilt of the defense's client. Again, the defense does not have to prove their theory or allegations in any way, shape, or form. It usually does not matter how farfetched their theories are, as long as an explanation is possible. If this effort puts sufficient doubt in the jurors' minds, the defense has done their job.

The defense attorney started his questioning of the detective in a courteous and respectful manner, however Sullivan knew this was a mirage. His motivation was to impress the jury with his courtesy and compassion, hoping that impression would be transferred to his client. Sullivan answered the defense attorney's questions in a slow and deliberate manner. After getting the preliminaries out of the way, the defense began to take a sarcastic and belittling attitude toward Sullivan in their questioning. The defense insinuated that Sullivan targeted Bridgeport as the person who committed this crime without looking or pursuing anyone else as a suspect. The defense began with its "is it possible" line of questioning, with their allegation that someone could have stolen Bridgeport's truck, committed the murder, and returned it back to the location where they took it, obviously without Bridgeport's knowledge or consent. Sullivan answered the only way he could…that it was possible, but very unlikely. Sullivan testified that he could find absolutely no evidence that this scenario ever took place. He added that there was nothing to support the supposition that Bridgeport's truck had been hijacked, or that some mysterious person(s), other than Bridgeport, tortured, raped, and murdered Beth Cowens.

Without going into detail, and just throwing out the notion for the jury to hear, the defense attorney asked Sullivan if he had ever heard or been aware of the fact that their client had been working with the federal government in reference to narcotics coming in from Texas. This was what the defense wanted the jury to hear; that Bridgeport was set up by the Texas dealers in retribution for helping the authorities. Sullivan answered that this scenario had come to his attention, and he had checked it out as far as was possible. He could find absolutely no substantiation or evidence that it ever happened.

The defense continued with their questioning, trying to prove negligence, incompetence, and almost downright dishonesty. Sullivan was questioned (interrogated) about the lack of physical evidence connecting their client directly to the murder of Beth Cowens and the lack of eyewitnesses. Sullivan, who had been down this road before, was prepared for almost every question he received. He felt like he testified as well and as honestly as possible. Sullivan felt confident but at the same time uncertain of what the end result was going to be.

CHAPTER SIXTEEN - A BARFLY AND HER TRAILER

Since it was getting close to quitting time after Sullivan finished his testimony, the judge dismissed the court proceedings for the day. The prosecutor, Archer, was staying at a Days Inn motel, which just happened to have a decent restaurant and lounge attached to it. The state was too tight to provide Sullivan with a motel room. Harrison County was an hour ahead of Poland County, so Sullivan was looking at a two-and-a-half hour drive home. Not exactly wanting to hit the road, he improvised and made arrangements to stay in the prosecutor's room (no gay jokes, please).

Sullivan and Archer graduated to the lounge for a few drinks before dinner. There they discussed the status of their case and their expectations for the next few days. Both calculated the trial would last the entire week, and hoped to have closing arguments concluded by Friday at the latest.

After several adult beverages, Harry and the prosecutor headed to the dining room to partake in a good evening meal. After dinner, Archer said he was going to go to his room and go to bed. He was generally not much of a night owl. Harry, however, who was always the party animal and usually the 'last dog to die,' decided to go back to the lounge and have a few more.

Harry happily walked in to see a country band playing. He just couldn't get into the current pop music of 1980. After ordering his drink, he noticed a few, unattached, middle-aged women who were size fourteens, trying to fit into size four skirts. They wore cowboy boots that nearly came up to their knees. Harry liked that look. Almost all of them had bleached blond hair and looked like they were out for a good time. *That's just what the doctor ordered*, Harry thought to himself. Not only was Belinda far away, physically speaking, but tonight the same distance existed in Harry's mind and heart as well.

Harry lit a Winston cigarette and slowly inhaled the tobacco smoke deep into his lungs. Even though he did not like to admit it, times like these were what Harry *really* enjoyed in life—smoking a cigarette while drinking an intoxicating drink at a dingy bar that housed a few barflies who obviously were not in their rookie year of barflying (a brand new word just got created there).

Harry saw three of the previously-described, young ladies setting at one particular table. He could not help but notice one of them giving him more than a casual glance. The one that was looking him over appeared to be a tad older than the other two. Harry, far from being picky, did not mind that at all. He was thrilled to have someone looking his way. Like Margaret before her, this lovely lady appeared to have more than an adequate set of breasts on her, and a behind that covered the entire bottom of the padded wooden chair she was so delicately resting that big, beautiful caboose on. A pattern was developing here.

The band slowed things down for a bit and began playing "Lookin' For Love" by Johnny Lee. The song fit Harry's intentions to a tee. He *was* looking for love in all the wrong places, at least for one night anyway. With the looks thrown his way, added to the mid-tempo song, indicated to Harry that this was his moment to act (pounce). He got up from his bar stool and walked over to this lady of the night. Harry quickly glanced to see if she had a wedding band on her left hand. It wouldn't have mattered much whether she wore one or not. If she was okay being in the company of a man who was not her husband, then Harry could live with it too. Harry further rationalized to himself that her old man was probably a prick anyway. Why else would she be at this lounge instead of at home? Besides, if Harry did not take advantage of the situation, somebody else most definitely would. Men are pigs.

The woman responded that she would love to dance with Harry. Together, they practically floated onto the wooden dance floor. Harry and the young maiden, who appeared to be in her late-forties, began the usual customary conversation—who they were what they were doing there.

Her name was Gretchen Portis of the nearby small town of English, Indiana. She was a hairdresser married to an over-the-road trucker who was seldom home. The fact that Harry was a state police detective usually was an advantage in the woman department rather than being a hindrance. He confessed to Gretchen that he was married too, but he and his wife were separated. Harry practically believed this as being the truth because he was seldom home for family time. Harry knew his wife, like most women that he experienced in his life, did not give a rat's ass about him anyway. Harry and Belinda were really beyond arguing. They simply did not have much of anything to say to each other when they were in each other's presence. In reality, there were four reasons Harry was not divorced:

1) His children and the pain it would cause them.
2) The financial burden it would create for everyone involved.
3) He was used to the routine of his lousy life.
4) Would the grass be greener on the other side?

Harry had a few more friendly dances with Gretchen before the band finally closed up for the night. Gretchen suggested Harry follow her home, as her husband was gone, and they could continue their newfound friendship. Harry agreed and followed her out to the parking lot. Gretchen got into her rusted-out Chrysler convertible with masking tape over the cracks in the top.

He followed her for a twenty minute drive to the outskirts of English, Indiana to what Harry jokingly described as a Southern Indiana estate—a dingy, singlewide mobile home. Leading the way to this Taj Mahal was a gravel driveway and a crumbling set of concrete steps to get into the front door. There was a built-on wooden deck located on the backside of the trailer. On the deck was a charcoal grill. Inside was an old refrigerator that kept their cheap beer cold. Even though it might not have seemed like it, Gretchen actually had all of the necessities of a simple life. Harry followed his newfound love inside. Surprisingly, it was clean and well-furnished.

    Gretchen fixed Harry one last drink while he sat down on her fake leather couch and lit up another cigarette. After some drunken small talk, she excused herself and stepped into the back bedroom. As Harry took a deep drag, he thought that maybe life was not so bad after all. With all the crap an individual has to put up with in life, there was still hope at the end of the day. After all, here was Harry, about to have sex…with an actual breathing human being. That in itself was practically a miracle.

    All of a sudden, Gretchen came out of the bedroom in the dim light of the mobile home. Maybe it was the booze or the crappy lighting, but to Harry, she looked *spectacular*. She was wearing a push-up bra with the nipples cut out, a pair of black bikini underwear, a garter belt with mesh hose, and a pair of spiked high heels. How did she know that was Harry's favorite outfit?

    Gretchen had an old-time country record playing to set the mood. Suddenly, everything in Harry's world was absolutely perfect. She may have been a middle-aged woman with bleached-blond hair living in English, Indiana, but she knew how to set up the atmosphere for a night of passion (in Harry's opinion, anyway)!

    At first, Harry worried about Gretchen's truck driving husband walking in the front door with a shotgun in hand, ready to kill the no-good son-of-a-bitch who was deflowering his bride. All of that fear and apprehension suddenly disappeared once Gretchen walked out in that outfit.

    Harry opened his bloodshot eyes to see 7:02am on the alarm clock. Even though Harry had a throbbing headache and could have easily slept another six hours, he knew he *had* to get out of bed. Harry, being the dedicated guardian of truth, justice, and the American way, recognized his presence in the courtroom was expected. He wanted to do anything and everything in his power in order to send Tater Bridgeport to prison for the rest of his life for his dastardly acts. Harry struggled into Gretchen's small, standup shower and lathered up. Before he left, Harry unapologetically applied some of Gretchen's husband's English Leather cologne, and left the not-so-innocent, but yet beautiful (to Harry) Gretchen asleep between the fouled sheets of her bed.

CHAPTER SEVENTEEN - THE TRIAL (PART II)

The day's testimony was going to include the police personnel who processed the scene, and the forensic pathologist who conducted the autopsy on Beth Cowens. The first witness was the ISP officer who processed the scene, followed the body to the morgue in Morganville, and photographed the autopsy. Joe Rallings testified as to the following:

1) The murder scene in general.
2) Evidence recovered.
3) Evidence recovered from the El Camino.
4) Autopsy photographs.
5) Results of lab analysis of evidence recovered such as fingerprints, blood, hair, and bodily fluids.
6) The initial identification of the victim as a white female.

His testimony lasted a couple of hours, and essentially tied Bridgeport's truck to the victim, as much as was possible at the time considering the technology that was available in the forensic sciences and medical technology. Most of the testimony was routine, which did not allow the defense to counter any of it. In other words, it was what it was, and nothing was going to change the results that the examinations and comparisons indicated.

After Officer Rallings testified, several other lab people from the state police testified as to the results of their examinations of the evidence that was presented to them for analysis and comparison. The next witness was the forensic pathologist that conducted the autopsy. His testimony was mostly technical in nature. He testified to the cause of death and the injuries that were received by the victim. The defense, of course, objected to most of the testimony of the pathologist, and especially to the photographs of the victim. They stated that the only purpose was to inflame the jury and to prejudice the jury against their "innocent" client. The judge overruled the defense's objections for the most part, and allowed the photographs into evidence. The jury was allowed to look at and study the photographs, for strictly probative reasons, of course.

After the pathologist finished his testimony, it was getting late in the day, so the judge decided to end proceedings and begin the next morning at 8am. Things were pretty much going as scheduled. The state only had two main witnesses left. They were *very* important because they put Beth Cowens and Tater Bridgeport together the night she was murdered.

The next day, the first witness to testify was the body man who told Sullivan that the chrome strip he was shown probably came off of a lime green El Camino or a Ranchero sport pickup truck. He explained why he identified the chrome strip as probably coming off of one of those type vehicles. His testimony was very important and brief. The defense really did not have many questions for him. The old saying in lawyerville is, *do not try to out-expert the experts, and know the answer to every question you ask before you ask it.* A good experienced attorney will follow this rule religiously.

The next witness called to the witness stand by the prosecution was the couple who observed Beth Cowens and Tater Bridgeport together driving through the city park together the very evening she later ended up dead. The defense did a lot of digging, trying to come up with reasons why one or both of these people had it in for Bridgeport. Sullivan did the same follow-up investigation in anticipation of the defense's efforts to provide an ulterior motive for this couple's testimony. Sullivan wanted to be 100% sure they were telling the truth. He was unable to come up with any reason for them to lie, or information that they had any connection to Bridgeport and Cowens.

As Sullivan stood in the "attorney's room" of the courthouse with Archer awaiting the start of court for the day, a deputy sheriff approached him.

"Harry, I have something here the sheriff instructed me to give to you."

He handed Sullivan the document. After a few seconds, Harry was surprised at what he was reading. They were divorce papers. He did not think his wife cared enough to bother filing, or even had the balls to take steps to end things. Harry really did not care at that point. He had not known what a real marriage was for several years. Harry was not immediately sure how he was going to be able to afford it. After all, he would have to pay for two attorneys, child support, and his own place. More than that though, he was worried about the effect it would have on his kids. Other than the financial part and his kids, he really could have cared a less. He figured he had been a piss-poor excuse for a husband and father anyway, so this could not do much more damage to his kids than Harry had already done in his fatherly endeavors.

"What is it?" Archer asked.

"Divorce papers from Belinda," Harry replied.

"Wow. Should I feel bad for you?" Archer wondered.

"No. It's been over for awhile. I just didn't think she had it in her to end things herself," Harry answered.

"Well, I'm sorry for the kids then," Archer offered.

"Me too," Harry responded.

The Judge called the court to order. It was hard for Harry to concentrate on the proceedings considering the paperwork he held in his hands. For the rest of the day, his attention was fifty percent at best. The prosecution called the next witness, Joe Broshears. Broshears calmly answered questions from the prosecutor regarding what he observed the evening in question. He confirmed the statement he gave Sullivan, in reference to observing Tater accompanied by Beth in Bridgeport's vehicle driving through the park. The prosecutor asked Broshears if he was positive about his identification, and he answered that he was.

It was time for the defense to question Broshears. The defense attorney asked if he knew Bridgeport or Cowens personally, or had ever had any personal dealings with either one of them. Broshears said he did not know Cowens at all, he just knew of her and who she was. He mentioned he knew who Bridgeport was, and knew him well enough to speak, but they only had a few conversations. Broshears explained it was just general conversation and nothing more. Broshears testified that he never had any personal dealings with Bridgeport of any kind. The defense asked if he had any reason to lie about Bridgeport or had any reason to try and get even with him.

"Absolutely not," answered Broshears.

The defense attorney realized that he would be unable to impeach Broshears's testimony. Further questioning would surely make him look desperate and appear as if he were badgering the witness. He had no further questions for Mr. Broshears.

The next witness was Linda Selbey. She testified to the same exact information that her boyfriend, Joe Broshears, testified to earlier. Her testimony was rather brief, and the defense did not even bother asking her any questions.

The other witnesses for the state included mostly law enforcement-related witnesses, who for the most part, played small roles in the investigation. However, their testimony was critical in order to put all the pieces of the puzzle together. The further along the trial went, the more confident Sullivan became about what the end result would be. It was his personal life that had an unsure future.

CHAPTER EIGHTEEN - WOMEN DRAMA

Harry left the courthouse and proceeded straight to the motel/lounge. He picked up the pay phone receiver and dialed his home number. The answer on the other end was the voice of his daughter, Holly.

"Hey, Honey, it's Dad."

"Hi, Dad. When are you coming home? We miss you!"

Being aware of the upcoming divorce, Harry held back the tears that were ready to fall.

"I miss you too. I'm working but I'll be home as soon as I can. Are you doing okay and minding your mother?"

Based on his brief conversation with his daughter, Harry concluded Belinda must not have told her anything about the situation. Based on how Holly acted on the phone, all was good in her little world.

"Is your mom there?"

Harry no more than got that question out of his mouth when he heard Belinda's unnerving voice on the phone.

"I had a feeling you might be calling me," Belinda sarcastically responded.

"Yeah, I got the divorce papers. I thought you might be decent enough to talk to me first before you did it," Harry replied.

"You're never home long enough to talk to you about anything. By the way, you've got a lot of nerve to even use the word 'decent' since you'll sleep with anything wearing a skirt!"

"If you don't get any at home, and what you occasionally get is like fucking a corpse, what do you expect?" Harry delicately inquired.

"Your clothes and other belongings are on the front lawn. The locks on the house have been changed. I'll see you in court!"

Harry heard a dial tone on the other end. That conversation did not go as planned. He knew trying to hang on to the marriage for the sake of the kids was fruitless. With that, Harry sauntered down to the lounge, sat down at the bar, lit up a Winston cigarette, and ordered a whiskey and ginger ale. He had not eaten all day, which was not unusual for him considering his schedule, so he started munching on the peanuts provided by the bar. Harry had just taken a sip of his intoxicating drink, when the defense attorney and his assistant walked into the lounge. Harry knew him. He really was not a bad guy as defense attorneys went. He sat down next to Harry and ordered a Manhattan.

"Harry, can I buy you a drink?" the defense attorney asked.

"No thanks. I'm afraid you might throw it up to me in court, and I don't want to be in debt to the enemy," answered Harry.

"Always the skeptic, huh, Harry?" the defense attorney wondered.

"Well, are you going to put your poor, misunderstood, innocent client on the stand and let him decry his innocence to the jury?" Harry wondered.

"I'm not sure yet. I am glad, however, to hear that you agree that Mr. Bridgeport is a poor, misunderstood, innocent man," the defense attorney agreed.

They both laughed at the exchange as the defense attorney walked away. Harry ordered another drink, the second of many sure to come. After a few minutes went by, he could not believe his eyes when his recently-made friend, Gretchen Portis, entered the bar. It became quickly obvious she was looking for love in all the wrong places…again. She approached him.

"Hey stranger, would you like to buy a girl a drink?"

"Sure, good lookin'. You're just what the doctor ordered. I'm in the mood to celebrate!"

"What's the special occasion?" Gretchen wondered.

"I just got divorce papers today," answered Harry.

It did not take long for the two, star-crossed lovers to end up back at Gretchen's "country estate." Harry's intuition told him to be on the safe side. He parked his unmarked police car on the side of the trailer, pointed toward the road in case he needed to make a quick exit. After all, Gretchen's husband was an over-the-road trucker who could come home at any time. Gretchen described him as a weekend drunk who beat her up on occasion. She planned on divorcing him when her financial situation improved. Looking around the premises, Harry doubted that the financial situation would get better anytime soon. He did not care how small or weak her husband might be. Harry knew the end of a .357 magnum pointed at him would make the angry husband look like the biggest and meanest man on the planet! Harry felt it was a good idea to avoid that situation as much as possible.

Harry walked outside with his alcoholic beverage and a cigarette. Gretchen soon followed with two Porterhouse steaks and baked potatoes to go along with them.

"Can you take care of these?" Gretchen inquired.

"I can take care of lots of things," Harry quickly answered.

As Harry began cooking on the husband's propane grill, he thought about how surreal all of this was. If only the husband knew that his expensive steaks were being grilled and soon eaten by an asshole that was going to stuff his wife full of dirty, filthy love later on. Harry shrugged it off and figured what the husband didn't know wouldn't hurt him.

Once the dirty deed was done, Harry and Gretchen lied in bed smoking cigarettes. A slight grumbling noise was heard coming from outside. It prompted Harry to think about his situation.

"When did you say your old man was supposed to be home?"

"What is today?"

"Uh, Thursday," Harry nervously answered.

"Sometimes when he deadheads, (drives home without a return load) he comes in on Thursday night rather than Friday night."

By now the grumbling noise sounded like a lion's roar. Knowing of what was about to take place, Harry jumped out of the bed, picking up whatever clothes that were in arm's reach. He quickly put on the clothes he was able to snag and exited out the back door of the trailer. Harry was missing his undershirt and one sock, but was not particularly worried about those at the moment. He was just happy to feel his keys and wallet in his pants pockets. Harry crept around to the south end of the trailer where his vehicle was parked, hidden by an old shed and a couple of trees. The burly husband exited his cab and walked towards his castle. Harry quietly slipped into his vehicle, turned the key, and furiously flew out of the driveway, like a saved soul out of the fiery depths of Hell.

CHAPTER NINETEEN - THE TRIAL (PART III)

It was time for the defense to start their part of the trial as the state rested. Sullivan wondered what approach they would take. Would they put Tater Bridgeport on the witness stand to testify? Would any of their witnesses perjure themselves? The defendant testifying had pros and cons. Sullivan's experience had been that more times than not the defendant chose not to testify. They are, of course, not required to thanks to the 5th Amendment. According to our system of justice, the accused carries the assumption of innocence until the prosecution proves them guilty beyond a reasonable doubt. That is always hammered into the jury's psyche by the defense every chance they get. However, two human nature truths hold true in almost every instance. First, a jury wants to hear a defendant testify and declare his innocence, giving his version of the facts and events. Second, a juror cannot simply forget something he heard from the witness stand, even though the judge instructs them to disregard it.

There are dangers to the defense if the accused testifies. It is almost open season on he/she as far as questioning by the prosecution. An average person goes up against an experienced, intelligent attorney...who do you think usually wins that debate? Adding to that, most of the time, the criminal history of the defendant usually is fair game. It does not give the defense points when their client has a rap sheet a mile long.

The intelligence, coolness, and ability to communicate effectively are very important in a defendant who chooses to testify. These characteristics and more have to be analyzed by the defense before a decision is reached whether a defendant should or should not testify. Guilty verdicts have been reached in numerous cases when the defendant testifies and does more damage to his cause than he does to improve it. However, although it has been proven to be rare, a few defendants have "pulled their chestnuts out of the fire" and the jury reached a favorable verdict for the defendant based sometimes solely on his/her testimony. So this is a very important decision the defendant and his attorneys have to make concerning how they proceed during their part of the trial.

The first witness the defense called was the mother of Tater Bridgeport. Led by the defense attorney and obviously well-rehearsed, she tried to come off as the grieving mother of a boy she tried to raise the best she could under very difficult circumstances. Those circumstances were, of course, mostly the fault of Bridgeport's father, making it almost impossible for him to develop as a normal youngster. Although Mrs. Bridgeport managed to conjure up a tear or two during her testimony, she finally got to the crux of her testimony.

She was asked about the discrepancy in what she told Detective Sullivan the morning he came to her house to question her about her son. She said she was intimidated, confused and panicked. Therefore, she simply made an honest mistake in what she told the detective. After really thinking things over, she realized it was between midnight and 1am when she heard her son drive his truck onto the driveway of her front yard. She heard him shut off the engine, close his vehicle door, then open the front door to the house. She even remembered him yelling at her in what she described as sort of a loud whisper that he was home. She told him no matter what time it was, she always wanted him to let her know when he got home because she worried. Mrs. Bridgeport remembered looking at the clock and seeing that it was a little after midnight.

Mrs. Bridgeport also testified that her boy was really a good boy who frequently helped her around the house, mowing grass, repairing things, etc. There was no way her boy would commit this horrible crime. She expressed sorrow for the Beth Cowens family and hoped that the police would do their job correctly and find the *real* guilty individual(s) who committed this crime. Mrs. Bridgeport appeared as a reasonably intelligent and sincere mother who loved her son, and would stand by him to the end. It was obvious to Sullivan that Mrs. Bridgeport had been schooled very well in her testimony. In reality, she made a very competent and believable witness. Incidentally, she added that she knew for a fact her son always left his key in the ignition to the unlocked truck. He was just a trusting person, after all.

Bridgeport sat there with a short, conservative haircut. He was even dressed in a better suit-and-tie than Sullivan could afford! That might not have been saying a lot, considering a detective's salary. Meanwhile, Sullivan's blood practically boiled. He knew Bridgeport for who he really was. He hoped that the jury would realize what bullshit the entire testimony was, and that there was not one iota of truth in it anywhere.

The defense finally looked at the judge and said, "No more questions for this witness, your honor."

It was now time for the prosecution to hammer Mrs. Bridgeport with inquisitive questions. It was like walking a tightrope to question an elderly woman who looked like Mother Hubbard. The prosecuting attorney did not want to lean too far on either side of the tightrope. If he did, it would come off as harassment of an old woman. Sympathy was something the prosecution wanted for their side, not the other way around. However, the prosecuting attorney had to do his best to convince the jury that she absolutely was not telling the truth. She was saying what she was saying in order to help her only son and save him from the unfriendly confines of prison.

Archer began his questioning by getting the witness to testify how much she loved her son. He tried to frame the questions in a way that would cause her to leave the impression that she loved her son so much that she would lie for him in order to keep from being convicted and sent to prison. Mrs. Bridgeport apparently was prepared for this line of questioning because she answered in a firm "no" that she would not lie for her son under any circumstances.

The prosecution then questioned her about what she told Detective Sullivan the morning that she talked to him, before she had an opportunity to talk to her son or his attorney. She repeated the same story that she was so intimidated, scared, and confused that she really did not know what she told the detective. Not wanting to call Sullivan a liar, she meekly testified that if the officer said what she said that morning, then she guessed she must have. When Archer wondered how her memory could be better several months after the murder than it was the day after, she calmly testified that again, she was scared, intimidated, and confused. Same old story. Archer inquired if it was true that she only changed her story after she conferred with her son and his counsel in order for her testimony reference the time he returned home to match her son's timetable, thereby providing him with an alibi. Her response was a simple "no."

Archer, figuring he did all he could do to impeach her testimony without getting on the verge of giving the defense attorney a chance to object claiming the prosecution was badgering the witness, ended his questioning of Mrs. Bridgeport. The prosecutor looked at the judge and advised him he had no more questions for this witness.

The next witness called by the defense was sort of a surprise, even though he was on the witness list. Federal witnesses who were involved in highly classified cases could usually get a federal judge to override a state subpoena just by ruling the case the federal officer was working on was a highly sensitive case with possible national security implications. By testifying, it would put federal officers in danger if they testified in a local or state prosecution. However, in this case the federal government did not go that route. They allowed their agent to honor the subpoena and appear in court ready to take his place on the witness stand. That decision would obviously result in bad relations between federal and state law enforcement agencies. Occasionally though, the Feds feel their agents' testimony is worth the possible consequences. Even at that, their testimony is often selective and regulated in the questions they will be required to answer. If they testify for the defense, some sort of a deal has usually been hashed out. In this particular case, an agreement was made that Bridgeport would co-operate fully with the federal government, and would testify in their pending cases that he had been involved in. In other words, sometimes the ends justified the means as far as the federal authorities were concerned. After all, the federal government is like a five hundred pound gorilla in the room—it does anything it wants to.

The defense called DEA Agent Dale Cunningham to the witness stand. Cunningham answered some preliminary questions concerning who he was and what he did. The defense asked him if he was familiar with the defendant in this trial, Larry "Tater" Bridgeport. Cunningham answered that he was. The defense attorney asked the DEA agent what the circumstances were, and how he knew Bridgeport. He responded that Bridgeport had been working with the federal government as an informant in a rather large drug investigation. In doing so, he agreed to testify against certain individuals who had been charged and arrested for being the source of illegal drugs coming into the Southern Indiana area. Bridgeport's assistance had been essential in getting the evidence against these subjects. His testimony would be imperative if convictions were to be achieved. Cunningham was asked if he was familiar with the charges and circumstances surrounding this particular case that Bridgeport was being tried for. He responded that he was aware of what Bridgeport had been charged with, but he was not familiar with the details of the case. The defense asked Cunningham in the course of his investigation if he heard any information about these individuals whom Bridgeport would be testifying against. According to Bridgeport's legal beagles, these were the men that were conspiring to frame Bridgeport for something in order to discredit any testimony he might offer against them. Cunningham started to say 'yes' when the prosecution objected as hearsay. The judge overruled the objection and the agent answered the question. He responded that he heard rumors from informants and word on the streets was that this was true. Bridgeport was going to be eliminated one way or the other in order to shut him up. The defense attorney asked him if he knew or had heard any details reference what was being planned in reference to eliminating Bridgeport. Cunningham replied that he did not know or had heard no details in regards to that. The defense attorney asked him one, final hypothetical question.

"Would you think it is likely that these individuals would be so desperate or devious as to set Mr. Bridgeport up by stealing his vehicle, committing a murder, then return the truck back to where they had stolen it, in order to make Mr. Bridgeport look like the murderer?" the lead defense attorney inquired.

Archer stood up and loudly objected advising the judge this was not only a leading and hypothetical question, but no preliminary grounds had been presented to the court to even justify the question. The judge granted the objection and Cunningham did not get the chance to express his opinion to this question. The problem was that the jury heard the idea or allegation, which gave them something to think about as far as a "possible" explanation of how Bridgeport's truck could have been taken, falsely setting him up for the murder. The defense told the judge they had no further questions for this witness.

The prosecution began their questioning of the witness. Archer was *furious* that Cunningham would even agree to testify for the defense, whether they had pending cases that Bridgeport had allegedly helped them with or not. Archer asked Cunningham the identity of these persons he heard these rumors from and where they were located. Cunningham said he could not answer that question due to a federal court order which prohibited him from answering questions about persons involved in a federal investigation. Archer made a motion and asked the judge to order the agent to answer his question. The judge, looking dumbfounded, said he needed to take a recess to research this motion.

Therefore, the judge discontinued the morning session of the trial early for the noon lunch break. He called the defense attorneys, Archer, and Cunningham back into his chambers. Sullivan was not invited to the party, so he went across the street to a local restaurant to grab a bite to eat.

When Sullivan returned to the courthouse for the afternoon session, Archer was still fuming. He told Sullivan that the judge actually telephoned the federal judge who allegedly gave the order that Cunningham was not to answer certain questions revealing the names of suspects, informants, or anything else of a pertinent nature in reference to the federal investigation. Archer said the local judge decided that he would not try to overrule a federal judge. Therefore, he ruled Cunningham did not have to answer the prosecutor's question. That decision really limited Archer on what he could ask Cunningham, and hampered his effort to impeach the agent's testimony. If Archer was going to have his hands tied, he was not going down without at least kicking.

"Agent Cunningham, can you give this court proof of any kind, one iota of evidence, other than rumors and supposed vague information from alleged informants, that any person or persons involved in or connected with your federal investigation had anything to do with the murder of Beth Cowens?" Archer wondered.

"No, I cannot," Cunningham had to confess.

"Would you admit or deny that an agreement was reached with Mr. Bridgeport by the federal government, that if you testified in this particular case, Mr. Bridgeport would testify in the pending drug cases where Mr. Bridgeport assisted the government in their investigations?"

"Yes, that agreement was made in my presence between Mr. Bridgeport, his attorneys, and a federal prosecutor," Cunningham responded.

"Did you or any other federal official, as far as you know, make at least one single inquiry to confirm if any of these supposed rumors or information given by alleged informants were true or had any element of truth?" Archer had to know.

"No, I did not make any inquiries into this nor did anyone else, to the best of my knowledge," Cunningham confessed.

"Did you or anyone else to your knowledge pass any information on to Detective Sullivan so he could follow up on them to substantiate or discredit these alleged rumors?" Archer expertly asked.

"No, that was not done either."

"Why?"

"Because we felt there was no real credibility to these rumors and it would be a waste of time. Plus, we do not allow state authorities to get involved in a federal investigation," Cunningham answered.

With that, Archer ended his questioning. The defense, looking somewhat dejected, called a few more witnesses. They were character witnesses for Bridgeport. They testified to what a good and honorable man Bridgeport was. Sullivan knew the defense was getting close to the end of their witness list. He wondered if they were going to put Bridgeport on the stand. Sullivan got his answer when he heard the defense attorney say to the judge that they were resting. The judge immediately dismissed the court for the weekend, and set final arguments for Monday morning. Sullivan was glad this whole thing was coming close to its conclusion.

CHAPTER TWENTY - THE BEAUTY AND THE BEAST

Harry knew he had to go home, at least in the general vicinity of home, in order to see his kids, get his belongings, and find a place to stay. He knew he would have to make a court appearance sometime in the near future so temporary financial arrangements could be made. After all, Harry's wife did not work and he knew he would have to pay her subsistence until the divorce was finalized. Indiana did not have alimony, only child support. Harry figured his wife would want everything but the kitchen sink. Just like the Jerry Reed song states, Harry feared she would get the goldmine, and he would surely get the shaft. Indiana also was a no-fault divorce state, meaning the court was only interested in the financials, property, and custody arrangements. They would not hear anything in regards to who did what, or who was at fault in the marriage. Indiana certainly was not California by any stretch of the imagination. Even if it were, Harry did enough to justify Belinda getting her fair share.

Harry drove up to his soon-to-be former residence and could not believe his eyes. Every article of clothing he owned, including his underwear and socks, were spread all over the front yard. They were not even folded and organized, just tossed across the grass. He tried going in, but the locks were changed; so he knocked instead. His charming and estranged wife answered.

"Get your clothes, mail, and leave the property. I'll see you in court," Belinda calmly stated.

"Can I at least see the kids?" Harry wondered.

"No, you can't see the kids. If I need to, I'll get a restraining order. Any communication between you and I will be through my attorney," Belinda informed Harry.

With that, Belinda slammed the door in Harry's face. It was clear that Belinda had her fill, especially with Harry hitting the bars on an almost nightly basis. Belinda wasn't dumb. She most likely knew Harry had his fill too and started ending up in the arms of other women. Harry proceeded to pick up his clothes, put them in his trunk and sped away, to where he was not sure. He ended up going to a local motel that had weekly rates. This dump was frequented mostly by out-of-town laborers who came into the area to work and needed lodging while they were in town. Harry rented a room and paid for two weeks in advance so he would be sure to have a roof over his head. With the stress of the trial, his nightly activities from the previous week, and the pressure caused by his recent divorce procedures, he found himself mentally exhausted. After getting to his room, he laid down on the bed to rest just for a few minutes, and immediately fell asleep. Harry slept straight through the evening and night, and awoke the next morning around daylight.

Harry stepped into the stripped-down shower and turned the water on as hot as he could stand it. He stood there for awhile, trying to not only clean his body, but somehow purify and cleanse his mind and spirit. It seemed Harry's whole life was consumed with felons of one stripe or another. He sometimes thought it must rub off because he often felt more akin to the lowlife trash of society that he dealt with day in and day out than the normal elements of the everyday world. Harry already notified the state police post of his new temporary residence and phone number.

Harry no more than got out of the shower when the phone rang in his hotel room. He picked it up thinking and hoping it was one of his kids. Instead, it was that of a female voice that he immediately recognized. Harry was kind of surprised to hear from Diana.

"How are you doing?" Diana inquired.

"A little hurt and lonely since I haven't heard from you in so long," Harry sweet-talked.

"I know you've been busy with the murder trial. I've been keeping up with it in the newspaper."

"Yeah, it's almost over, thank God," Harry confessed.

"I also read in today's paper that you're getting a divorce," Diana offered.

"Court records, huh? Yeah, Belinda finally did what I should have done a few years ago," Harry admitted.

"I thought you might need a good friend to talk to. I'm concerned about you and often wonder how you're doing considering the pressure of your job," Diana said.

"Well, I guess I'm doing okay, considering the circumstances," Harry replied.

"After I found out you were getting a divorce, I called a few of your friends to find out where you were staying. Do you want to get together tonight? I'd love to see you. We could meet somewhere in Morganville."

"Where's your husband?" Harry wondered as he took a swig from his bottle of cheap whiskey.

"Where do you think?" Diana responded.

Harry did not think much of himself as a human being, much less a lady's man. He could not for the life of him figure out why Diana even gave him a second thought. She was one of those women whom Harry always thought was completely out of his league. Harry knew Diana was a really nice, classy person. He did not want to drag her down into the muck of life that he currently resided in. Harry was just happy to be out with a good friend where they could enjoy each other's company and forget their problems for awhile. It did not hurt that Harry was headed to a place where the continuation of his ever-growing alcohol problem could be sustained.

Doria's Corral Club was a nice country and western restaurant/bar. The steaks served there were the best around. Harry arrived a few minutes early. Considering whom he was meeting, Harry normally would have been nervous but he was half-buzzed from drinking in the car on the way there. After ordering his usual drink, Harry thought about how this scenario was increasingly repeating itself—drinking and meeting a woman at a bar. At least this one he personally knew prior to entering the establishment.

Diana walked in the side door. To say she looked striking would be an understatement. She just carried herself like a woman should. Everything about her shouted class. Diana wore a pair of form fitting jeans, with spike heeled black boots. Her shirt was of the buttoned down, red silk variety that was somehow tucked into her tight jeans. Diana was the kind of woman who could make an old rag wrapped around her look stylish.

Harry immediately waved her over and they proceeded to a table. He pulled her chair out and she reached over to give him a flirty kiss as she sat down. Harry could not restrain himself.

"My God, Diana, you look fantastic!" Harry emphatically stated.

They spoke as if they had not seen each other, 'since fifteen years ago,' as the Conway Twitty song went. She ordered a vodka martini, shaken not stirred. Harry was so thrilled to be having an actual conversation with a woman he liked and respected he could hardly hide his excitement. He spent years speaking to Belinda, but nothing of substance was ever said.

After dinner and several alcoholic beverages, the band began playing. The third song they played was the George Jones all-time favorite, "He Stopped Loving Her Today." To Harry, this was the greatest, all-time favorite "belly-rubber" song ever recorded. This was slowly turning into the best day Harry had in years.

"Would you like to dance?" asked Harry.

"Well, sure," Diana answered.

With her heels on, she was almost as tall as Harry. Diana wrapped her arms around Harry so tight it was as if she were holding on for dear life. Her perfume was not of the dollar store variety like Gretchen (Harry's previous conquest) before her. Their eyes met as Diana moved her hand behind Harry's head. She moved her lips to his ear and softly whispered, "I think I'm ready."

"Ready for what?" Harry wondered.

"Ready to leave my husband," Diana replied.

"I thought you meant something else," Harry laughed.
"Don't get too ahead of yourself, Cowboy," flirted Diana.
"Has it gotten that bad?"
"It's more than that."
"What else is going on?" Harry asked.
"My feelings for you," Diana answered.

Harry was genuinely taken aback. He never felt like he was a handsome man. He slept with women whose best days were *at least* ten years behind them and that was being kind. Harry cussed like a sailor and made a miniscule salary. He could not fix a thing around the house unless it could be taken care of with duck tape. No one would ever mistake Harry for a sharp dresser either…or a rocket scientist for that matter. What in the world was she thinking? Even though Harry had the mental capacity of a *very* intelligent ape, he was smart enough not to question her feelings too damn much.

The door to the cheap motel room flung open. Harry and Diana kiss passionately while walking, attempting to make it towards the bed. Harry barely bothered closing the door. It stayed cracked. The only light was from the outside street lights shining in through the window. Both fall on the bed and continue their make-out session. Harry stopped for a second and looked closely into Diana's eyes.

"I'm in love with you," Harry confessed.
"I feel the same," Diana responded.

Harry Kissed Diana gently. After years and years of being completely miserable, Harry finally felt happy and at ease.

CHAPTER TWENTY ONE - THE TRIAL (PART IV): THE VERDICT

It was Monday morning and Sullivan left early for the two hour drive over to Harrison County. There was practically a skip in his step upon arriving at the courthouse from the night before with Diana. Even though he was in the middle of a divorce, he could not remember being happier. Once inside, Sullivan asked Archer if he spent the entire weekend preparing his final argument. Archer pointed to the side of his head.

"It's all in here Harry, right in the vault. Besides, I was busy this weekend."

"What kept you busy?" Sullivan wondered.

"The usual…drinking beer, mowing grass," answered Archer.

Archer had four acres that he mowed religiously…and enjoyed Budweiser a little *too much*.

The judge called the proceedings to order. The prosecution got to make the final argument first, and then the defense had their turn. The prosecution then got a rebuttal to counter what the defense said in their final argument. This appears to be, and is, an advantage given to the prosecution, mainly because they have the obligation to prove the defendant's guilt beyond a reasonable doubt. The defense has an obligation to prove nothing. This is one of the many important facets of how the United States' system of justice operates.

Archer got up first and began his final argument. It was similar to the ones Sullivan heard him give on previous occasions. He basically went over the testimony and evidence presented in the courtroom which pointed to Bridgeport's guilt. He reminded the jury that Beth was only fourteen years old, really just a child in a woman's body. Archer was obviously trying to tug on some heart strings here. He concluded by stating nothing could bring Beth back or undo the horrible things that had been done to her. However, it would be a measure of justice and not revenge to convict Bridgeport of this crime. Archer thanked the jury for their time and patience in hearing this unpleasant case, and took his seat. His closing argument was essentially Attorney 101, but it was about as good as Archer got.

The defense attorney then stood up and began his final plea. The first thing he did was thank the jury on behalf of his client for listening to the evidence closely and keeping an open mind. He then asked the jury to hold it against him and not his client if he had said anything during the proceedings that was negative concerning the juror's opinion or feelings toward his client. Defense attorneys usually use this little ruse in order to appear to be the humble underdog. He then began his characterization of the evidence and the case in general, reminding the jury that his client had nothing to prove. It was clear that this was his justification for his client not taking the witness stand. His approach to the case was agreeing that what happened to Beth Cowens was terrible beyond words. However, the only thing almost equally as unthinkable would be to convict the wrong man.

He explained the difference between a "reasonable doubt," and "preponderance of the evidence." This is the standard of proof required in a civil trial, as opposed to a criminal trial. He continued in that the preponderance of evidence meant that if it was more likely that something happened then did not happen, the juror was required to find that it did, in fact, happen. He explained that a reasonable doubt was a much higher standard of proof for obvious reasons. That was dealing with a person's freedom and his/her future. He then began with his characterization of the evidence. He did not deny that the state may have proven Bridgeport's truck guilty beyond a reasonable doubt. However, he assured the jury that the state failed to meet their burden of proof in proving Mr. Bridgeport guilty of this crime beyond a reasonable doubt. He then reminded the jury that if they decided the state had failed in their obligation or standard of proof which is, of course, beyond a reasonable doubt, that they were obligated to find Mr. Bridgeport 'not guilty.'

The defense attorney brought up and praised his client for helping the federal government get the drug dealers in the national drug trade at the cost of them framing his client for this unspeakable crime. According to Bridgeport's attorney, this was done in order to destroy Bridgeport's credibility and get him out of the way concerning his pending testimony against them. Even though there was no evidence to substantiate this allegation, the defense attorney told the jury that this in itself should provide sufficient reasonable doubt. The defense had a few more chosen criticisms of the investigation by the police and Detective Sullivan in particular, for conducting an incompetent, negligent, and unethical investigation. This resulted in the hurried and premature arrest of their client, Mr. Bridgeport.

In what was either a brilliant psychological move or basic desperation, the defense asked the jurors to consider the prospect of Mr. Bridgeport being their son. Would they approve of the rush to judgment that the police and the prosecution were obviously guilty of? The defense, almost in crocodile tears, asked the jurors to consult with almighty God for guidance before they came to a final decision. He even reminded them that Jesus himself was unfairly and unjustly hung on a cross for alleged crimes he was innocent of.

Sullivan feared that some of the jurors might be bleeding hearts or simply did not have the gumption to send someone to prison for the rest of their life. He also worried that they would fall for the defense attorney's psychological tricks.

The trial lasted approximately eight days, a little longer than Sullivan figured it would. Sullivan and Archer exited the courthouse and headed to the local Knights of Columbus Club to wait out the jury and indulge in several adult beverages. This was their routine after almost every trial they were ever involved in together. Sullivan did not know what to think about the forthcoming result of the trial. He believed they presented a good case with an abundance of circumstantial evidence.

Sullivan and Archer sat at the K of C Club for five hours when the phone rang. They had bloodshot eyes and were slightly wasted. The person on the other end of the phone was the court bailiff advising that the jury reached a verdict. Sullivan and the prosecutor immediately headed back to the courthouse, stumbling a bit on the way. The jury deliberated for just six hours. Considering one hour was allotted for dinner, five hours was not a very long time at all to consider a murder case. A quick verdict could mean good or bad news for both legal teams.

As Archer and Sullivan entered the courtroom it seemed like everyone was already there except for the jury. As soon as everyone was seated, the judge told the bailiff to bring the jury into the courtroom. During the entire trial, Sullivan made eye contact with a certain juror whom he felt would probably be the person selected as the jury foreman. He was a short man in his early fifties from the Philippines. Sullivan discovered later on that he was a freedom fighter during World War II. Knowing that he would have had to put his military experience on the initial questionnaire, Sullivan was amazed that the defense allowed this guy to remain on the jury. Chances were he was probably pretty hard-nosed and believed in old fashioned justice.

Sullivan noticed that the guy did not make eye contact with him as he walked in with the rest of the jurors. This caused the sweat to break out on Sullivan's forehead. He immediately knew that was not a good sign. The judge asked the foreman of the jury to identify himself, and sure enough it was the little Filipino guy. The judge asked him if the jury had reached a verdict, and he answered in the affirmative. The judge told Bridgeport and his attorneys to stand and face the jury.

"What say you on the offense of first degree murder?" asked the judge.

"Verdict. We the jury, in the above and title case, find the defendant, Larry Bridgeport, not guilty of first degree murder," stated the jury foreman.

In that instant, Sullivan felt his head get extremely hot. He really could not believe or translate in his mind the significance of what had just been said.

"On the lesser included offense of second degree murder, what say you?" asked the judge.

"Verdict. We the jury, in the above and title case, find the defendant, Larry Bridgeport, not guilty of second degree murder" responded the jury foreman.

Sullivan's head was quickly spinning with disbelief and confusion.

"On the lesser included offense of voluntary manslaughter, what say you?" asked the judge.

"Verdict. We the jury, in the above and title case, find the defendant, Larry Bridgeport, guilty of manslaughter" answered the jury foreman.

Sullivan looked over at the defense table. There appeared to be no visible response from Bridgeport or his attorneys. It was as if they did not know how to comprehend what had just happened either, what it meant, or what the long-term results would be. After a minute or so, the realization of the unfair sentence hit Sullivan like a ton of bricks. He started to stand up with the intention of shouting his protesting opinion to the jurors. His rational side took over and he sat back down, knowing nothing could change the verdict now.

How in the hell can the torture-murder of a fourteen year-old girl be manslaughter? That son-of-a-bitch is either guilty of first degree murder, or he's guilty of nothing!

Sullivan was obviously not the only one who was unhappy with the verdict. The noise level increased to a level that was not conducive to normal court proceedings. Seeing this, the judge immediately began banging his gavel and told everyone in the courtroom to sit down and get quiet or he would immediately clear the courtroom. He then asked the defense if they wanted to poll the jury. They advised they did. The judge then proceeded to ask every juror individually if this was their true and accurate verdict. Each juror answered in the affirmative. The judge then thanked the jury for their service and dismissed them. He set a date for sentencing and ordered a pre-sentence investigation to be conducted by his court personnel. With that, he ended the proceedings, and everyone exited the courtroom.

Detective Sullivan felt angry and disgusted with the end result. Yes, he was found guilty of something, but it was much less than what he was really guilty of. There certainly was no victory dance between Sullivan and Archer at the K of C Club afterwards. A conviction of manslaughter for a torture-murder like this seemed like a poor definition of any kind of true justice. Where was the justice for Beth Cowens? That girl never even made it into adulthood.

Sullivan knew the *maximum* sentence for manslaughter was twenty years. Chances were Bridgeport would never do that much time. In state courts, sentences allowed a convict to receive one day off his/her sentence for every day served, as long as they stayed out of trouble. In other words, even *if* Bridgeport got the maximum sentence, he would probably be out in ten years. Making matters worse, his sentence would be considered served in full. The state could not even keep him on probation. By his release date, he would still be a relatively young man. Meanwhile, Beth Cowens would be nothing but bones six feet under.

Sullivan felt like he had to find out what was going on in that jury deliberation room. With his detective skills, he found out the contact number of the jury foreman. He knew he was not supposed to do that, but he really did not give a damn at that point. He contacted the Filipino man and asked him if he would be willing to meet him for a cup of coffee, to which he readily agreed.

They met at a local diner. Sullivan shook his hand and they ordered two cups of coffee. The first thing Sullivan made clear was that he was not there to criticize or pass judgment. He just had to know what the jury was thinking when they found Bridgeport guilty of manslaughter in a torture-murder.

The jury foreman, named Jose Padina, said the first jury count taken was nine to three—nine favoring guilt on the first degree murder charges. Three jurors were for 'not guilty' on all charges. That is how good the defense team was; especially spectacular considering they were public defenders and not big money hired guns. Mr. Padina said that count never changed throughout the deliberations. The three voting for 'not guilty' were the only women on the jury. Mr. Padina said their argument was that the state had not proved Bridgeport actually committed the murder beyond a reasonable doubt. In their opinion, Bridgeport could have been set up by someone stealing his truck, committing the rape and murder, and returning the truck to Bridgeport's residence where they originally stole it, thereby framing him for the murder. Everyone agreed that:

1) Bridgeport had a relationship with Beth Cowens.
2) Bridgeport was with her the evening before she was killed.
3) Bridgeport's truck was obviously involved in the crime.

However, the three female jurors brought up that although she was only fourteen years of age, Beth was clearly a drug user and a "tramp." As outrageous as it sounds, they almost insinuated that she may have gotten what she deserved. Mr. Padina confessed there was no changing the women's opinions or votes. If they had not come back with the verdict of guilty on the lesser-included offense of manslaughter, it would have been a hung jury at best. He apologized to Sullivan for how things worked out, and reiterated that was not the way he and eight of the other jurors wanted it to be. Mr. Padina also complimented Sullivan on the job he did on the investigation. He added that he knew of nothing Sullivan could have done differently or better that would have affected the outcome of the trial, short of a confession or an eyewitness.

Sullivan thanked him for his time and left the restaurant, still with a lump in his heart and his stomach. He was unable to rationalize how the three female jurors came up with the conclusion they came up with. Sullivan did not know if the defense would appeal or not. He felt like they would, even though they were already damn lucky, in Sullivan's opinion. Bridgeport dodged a bullet twice—once for avoiding the death penalty, and the second time for avoiding conviction on the first degree murder charge. Even considering that, looking at a twenty-year sentence probably appeared pretty intimidating to Bridgeport. For at least ten years, he would not be able to have sex (with a woman anyway), drink alcohol, or do drugs…not to mention, rape, torture, and kill more young girls. After giving it some thought, Sullivan surmised Bridgeport would likely appeal the decision.

CHAPTER EIGHTEEN – ONE LAST INTERVIEW

Detective Harold Sullivan could not shake the effects of this case like he had others. The girl was just too young. The crime was just too unspeakable. He kept questioning himself, *What could I have done differently?* He blamed himself for the results of the Cowens murder trial. In his opinion, it hurt his professional reputation and his personal pride in the job he did as an Indiana State Police detective. The end result was Sullivan losing interest in his work from that point on. The passion was simply gone and he was just going through the motions. To him, it was just a (small) paycheck from that moment on. His drinking did not get any better. Because of his piss poor attitude, Sullivan's relationship with his co-workers also suffered, especially with his boss (which had never been too good anyway). It actually turned into sort of a game where his boss tried to catch him doing something against state police regulations, like drinking while on duty, not doing a competent job on his cases, etc. However, Sullivan was able to stay out of Knapp's way enough to get by. His only real goal anymore was to survive for seven more years until he got his twenty years on the department to qualify for the state police pension. At that point, he would tell them to take the job and shove it!

Bridgeport was subsequently sentenced, as expected, to the maximum twenty years. He was sent to the Indiana Reformatory in Pendleton to serve out his sentence. He had been gone for about six months when Sullivan received a letter in the mail. It was from Bridgeport. It read as follows:

"Why don't you come up and see me? Maybe we'll play a little game of let's make a deal. Maybe I will tell you what might have happened out in that cornfield."

Sullivan laughed to himself. Bridgeport was truly an ignorant person. The verdict and sentence was already handed down. There were no more deals to be made. The plea bargain possibility was long gone. Archer would have looked like a fool, trying him and then turning around and writing a letter to the appeals court, asking for leniency of any kind. All Bridgeport could do with speaking to Sullivan was ruin his chances at a successful appeal. Sullivan was all for that so he made the necessary arrangements to interview Bridgeport one last time.

Upon arrival at the prison, Sullivan could not help but notice the imposing nature of the building. It was an old facility with tall grey walls that looked more like an old Mayan structure located somewhere in South America than it did a prison in the United States. Once Sullivan entered the prison, Sullivan identified himself and surrendered his service revolver to prison officials. He went into a room that was partitioned off by glass walls, as were other similar looking rooms. It was there where he waited patiently for Bridgeport. A prison officer finally brought Bridgeport into the room and sat him down at a table across from Sullivan. Sullivan already had a notepad and his tape recorder ready to record whatever Bridgeport had to say.

"You're looking good, Tater. It looks like prison life is agreeing with you," Sullivan lied.

"Yeah, well when you're caged up like an animal, for something you didn't do, I guess it makes you look fat and sassy," Bridgeport sarcastically replied.

"Well, I didn't come up here to talk about that. The jury has already spoken. As far as I am concerned you got off damned lucky to only get what you got. Now, what do you have to offer to me?" Sullivan wondered.

"What I am going to tell you is what *might* have happened. I will never testify to any of it as being the truth, unless the prosecutor agrees to petition the appeals court to give me a pardon or reprieve. I've got to get out of this fuckin' place, Sullivan!" Bridgeport pleaded.

"Well, I guess we have nothing to talk about then," Sullivan informed him as he began to get up out of his seat.

"You're going to leave? All right, fuck it. I'll tell you the truth then. I hope this eats at you and Archer, knowing you put the wrong guy in prison and let the real killer go," Bridgeport stated.

Sullivan sat back down and turned the tape recorder on.

"I'd been fucking Beth for several months. One night I took her to a party. Of course, she was all for it. You know how she was. There was supposed to be a bonfire that night out by the old bridge. It was sort of early when she got in the truck, so I decided to cruise around to bide some time. We smoked and drank for an hour or so," Bridgeport informed Sullivan.

"Did you see anyone you knew while you were riding around with Beth?" Sullivan asked.

"I was getting wasted pretty fast, but I don't really remember noticing anybody in particular. After riding around town for an hour or so, I saw Harry Seasons standing on the corner near where the IGA grocery store is located. He was smokin' a cigarette, hangin' out."

"Did you drive through the park just before dark, and if so, did you notice anyone you recognized as you were driving through the park?" Sullivan interrupted.

"I don't know if or when I went through the park. I might have, and probably did, but I don't remember. As I told you earlier, I don't remember seeing anyone. Anyway, like I was saying, I saw Harry and pulled over next to where he was standing. I asked him if he wanted to go to the bonfire. He got in and we drove out to the country. I guess it was around midnight when we drove out by the old bridge. We didn't see any bonfire or anything else for that matter. I guess the party got canceled and no one informed me of it. I pulled over. We just parked, listened to music, drank some Jack, and smoked some grass."

"You were still getting high around this time?" Sullivan inquired.

"Yeah, especially Beth. She just couldn't handle it like we could. We decided to move to a more out of the way location so we wouldn't be bothered by the pigs (police). I drove down the gravel road for a few more miles and noticed a lane off to the right that eventually ended at a cornfield. Harry already told me at the bridge while we were taking a leak that he wanted to fuck Beth."

"How did you feel about that, considering she was your girlfriend?" Sullivan wondered.

"I didn't give a shit. She wasn't my girlfriend; at least not in my eyes. I let him know he'd have to take sloppy seconds though. Harry grabbed the Jack Daniels and said he was going back to the tailgate. I started kissing Beth...nothing too romantic. Just a little bit in order to get her clothes off. She got naked and I pushed her head down so she could blow me. I made her suck my dick until I came in her mouth. She got pissed about that because I didn't tell her before I came and that I wasn't going to be able to satisfy her. I certainly wasn't going to go down on her. Not after I finished, I wasn't. I staggered out and went to the back of the truck. I told Seasons it was his turn. I sat on the tailgate, drinking more Jack and smoking a few cigarettes. I could hear Harry and Beth arguing. She finally screamed at him, telling him that she wouldn't fuck him if he was the last guy on earth. The next thing I heard were muffled sounds from Beth, and an occasional whimper. After several minutes, I heard Beth call Seasons a motherfucker, and that she was going to turn us in for rape, especially since she was only fourteen. The next thing I remember is Seasons saying she ran away. I kept a .22 semi automatic rifle on the back window of my truck. Seasons flipped the headlights on. I could see Beth as she started to run into the corn stalks. Seasons started chasing her into the cornfield with my rifle. The next thing I heard was a gunshot. I think there were around ten rounds shot by the time I got there. I could see Beth's naked body lying on the ground in one of the corn rows. Seasons told me I had to shoot her too to be a part of it. If I didn't, he'd kill me since I was the only eyewitness. He had the rifle in his hand, man. What was I supposed to do? I didn't want to die too. So, I took the gun and shot a few rounds at her until the clip was empty. I don't know if I hit her or not. When we came upon her body, we couldn't tell how many times she'd been shot. There was just blood all over her back. Seasons sort of kicked her to see if she reacted. She moaned so he went back to the truck and came back with a knife and a metal baseball bat that I kept in the truck. I asked him what he was gonna do now. I guess she offended him since she said she wouldn't fuck him. He was pissed, man."

"What'd he do next?" Sullivan asked.

"He took the knife and started carving diagrams on her back like squares and circles. I tried to stop him, but he ignored me. Each time he cut her she moaned a little. Then he grabbed the bat. He put the small end of it in her ass and rammed it up there as far as he could. He was a sick fuck, man. We weren't sure if she was still alive or not at that point. He grabbed the knife and bat and told me to pick up the rifle. I guess he didn't want me to have the weapons that could be used against him. Seasons told me to run over her just to make sure she was dead. I didn't want to and told him so. He said he would cut me and leave me out there with her if I didn't. So, I ran over her once. I had to. Otherwise he was going to kill me too. We left after that."

"What'd you do with the weapons?"

"On the way back to Glen Burnie, we went to the Wabash River Bridge and threw her clothes and my rifle in the river," confessed Bridgeport.

"Then what'd you do?" Sullivan inquired.

"I drove back to town and dropped Seasons off at his house. He told me on the way there that we had to keep it all secret. If I told anyone, he'd find me and do to me what he did to Beth. I had no choice, Sullivan. When I woke up, I wasn't sure if what happened really happened or not, ya know? I was out of it for a bit. A few hours later, I went to the liquor store and that's when I ran into you," Bridgeport said.

"Is there anyone or anything, such as physical evidence, or anything else that can confirm anything you're telling me?" Sullivan wondered.

"Maybe. I need you and Archer to get me released from this hellhole. I'd testify and cooperate one hundred percent," Bridgeport offered.

"Bridgeport, even if the account you gave is one hundred percent true and accurate, it doesn't mitigate your involvement. If the jury would've known what you've just admitted to in this interview, they would've no doubt found you guilty of first degree murder! It just means two of you were involved in the rape and murder of Beth Cowens, not just you. In other words, the implication of Seasons doesn't lessen your responsibility or involvement," Sullivan explained to him.

"Whatever, man. You tell the prosecutor unless he gets me out of here, this conversation never happened and everything I said was just a pack of lies. Seasons will get off scot free without my testimony. One more thing…I want you to know that I hold you responsible for me being in this shithole," Bridgeport informed Sullivan.

"You're the one responsible for you being in here, Bridgeport," Sullivan reminded him.

"I'll get even with you when I do finally get out of here," Bridgeport threatened.

With that, Harry Sullivan stood up and gathered his papers and tape recorder.

"You little motherfucker. If I see you on the same side of the street, if you don't immediately turn around and walk the other way, I'll drop you like a case of the clap! There isn't a jury in the country that would convict me of a damn thing. Don't you forget that," Sullivan warned Bridgeport.

A prison official came in and took Bridgeport back to prison population. Sullivan walked out of the glass enclosed room. On the way to his vehicle, Sullivan thought about what bothered him about Bridgeport. He was the kind of a sneaky son-of-a-bitch who would not face you head-on. He would be hiding behind a shrub some night with a shotgun waiting for you to come home and get out of your car. Sullivan had been threatened numerous times by people who were a lot bigger and badder than Tater Bridgeport, but none who were more mean and devious.

On the drive back, Sullivan's conscious got to bothering him the more he thought about this case. He knew Bridgeport was guilty and was exactly where he should be. Deep down though, he also knew that Harry Seasons was undoubtedly involved in this crime, but to what extent he was not sure. The question was how he could prove Seasons's involvement in this murder? It would be very difficult, even with Bridgeport's testimony and full cooperation. Without it, a conviction was virtually impossible. There was just no physical evidence linking Seasons to the crime. Sullivan hated to think about Seasons getting away with it completely. At the same time, he did not believe justice was served having Bridgeport serving only ten years. But what could he do?

Sullivan felt like a complete failure and definitely took it personally. He had secretly made a promise to Beth Cowens on that hot and humid day that he would get her justice. Deep down, Sullivan was a very tender guy who took his job very seriously, probably too much. It cost him his marriage. It made him an extremely bitter person, trusting and believing in no one. It resulted in him being on the verge of alcoholism (he might have already been there). It seemed every night he could see Beth Cowens's face, or what was left of it, in his sleep. It haunted him that he had been such an utter failure in getting her the justice that he promised her. This was the most important case in his career and the one that took the biggest toll on him. This case would haunt him the rest of his life. For all practical purposes, it also ended his effectiveness as a detective. Sullivan almost felt as if he were the one who was doing time for failing to avenge Beth Cowens's untimely death. That was a hard thing to live with, day in and day out.

EPILOGUE

The conclusion of the Beth Cowens murder case was certainly not what Sullivan wanted. In reality, it was a mixed blessing. He did get a conviction, but not the conviction that was warranted considering the evidence.

Sullivan took the interview with Bridgeport to Archer, and got the answer he expected. Without independent substantiation, corroboration, witnesses, evidence, etc., Bridgeport's statement was as worthless as tits on a nun. Sullivan did attempt to speak with Harry Seasons, but Seasons would not give him an interview. Incidentally, Seasons was later convicted on rape charges in another jurisdiction. Due to those charges, he received more than twenty years in prison. Sullivan was somewhat relieved about this turn of events. After all, what comes around goes around.

Bridgeport did serve his sentence, and apparently did a better job following the rules in prison than he did on the outside, because he served ten years with no additional time tacked on due to misbehavior. This was due to the *good time* provision in the Indiana law statutes.

Harry finally got his divorce from Belinda. He saw his kids regularly and they seemed to adjust about as well as could be expected. After a few years, he married his true love, Diana Kleemer. After retiring from the Indiana State Police, Sullivan started a private detective business, which was a good transition for him considering his former profession.

With Poland County being the small place it was, Sullivan was not surprised when he finally faced his former nemesis once he was released from prison. One night Harry and Diana went to a local bar to have a drink. An hour of good conversation went by when lo and behold, who should walk in, but Larry "Tater" Bridgeport, with two skanky-looking women at his side. Not knowing Harry was there, Bridgeport sat down directly across from him and Diana.

"Harry," Diana whispered.
"What?"
"Is that Bridgeport sitting over there?"
Harry looked over and saw an older-looking Bridgeport in the flesh. At first, Sullivan was a little concerned. He remembered Bridgeport's threat ten years ago. Adding to that was the fact that Sullivan's gun was in the glove compartment of his car.
"Yeah, that's him. Damn, he's aged!"
"Let's get out of here. I don't want any trouble," Diana pleaded.
"Not until I've finished my beer."
Once Harry downed his beer, they got up to leave. As Harry walked

by Bridgeport he stopped momentarily to look down at him. He recalled Bridgeport's threat ten years prior and what he did to fourteen year-old Beth Cowens. Any concern that was there initially went away immediately.

"You got anything you want to say to me?" Sullivan asked.

"No, sir," Bridgeport weakly answered.

With that, Harry and Diana walked out of the bar. A year or so later, Sullivan heard Bridgeport died of a heart attack while working at a local grain mill. Harry, although not a religious man, thought to himself that the good Lord imposed the final death sentence on Larry "Tater" Bridgeport. He would continue throughout eternity serving his sentence in the flames of Hell. After all, when it comes right down to it, God is the final judge and arbiter, not only for Larry Bridgeport, but for all of us.

The author, at his handsome best.

IN RETROSPECT

Since several copies of this novel have been purchased, and a new printing company will be releasing the book, some observations and comments seem in order from the author. In the second edition, the names of several characters have been changed completely in order to erase any question or suspicion of them being anything other than fictional characters. The reviews have been very positive from every person who has personally commented to the author after reading the book. However, it is understood that any person or persons who had criticisms of the work would either not say anything at all or go to the internet to express their views.

The reason for the necessity of obtaining a new publisher was due to complaints made to the previous publisher. For reasons of their own, the publisher decided to cease printing the novel. In reference to those criticisms, they were reportedly for two things: The content of the book and the quality of the writing.

In regards to the complaints concerning the content of the book, no apology will be made. It was never the intent of the author to shock, embarrass, or cause any unhappiness or emotional distress to anyone in the writing and publishing of this novel. As had been previously stated, this work was inspired by a gruesome homicide, investigated by the author many years ago when he was a detective.

As to the few negative comments posted online in regards to the writing, unless the persons doing the criticizing happen to be English or literature teachers, or are professional book critics, their criticisms will be received in the same vain they were given.

A clear warning was given in the introduction of the book in reference to the content, stating it was not recommended for the sensitive reader. If it were a movie, it would most certainly earn an 'R' rating. Also, this book was written in the language and environment that the author worked and lived in during that particular time in his life. The personal stories and events of all characters in the novel are fictional and never actually took place as far as the author is aware of. They are for the sole purpose of creating a storyline which would lead to compelling reading. As far as the murder itself, the subsequent murder investigation, the arrest, trial, conviction, and incarceration, that part of the book was written from the memory of the author. No reports, notes, newspaper articles, or court documents were referred to.

Since the actual homicide investigation did in fact inspire the writing of this book, it would be untrue to say there are absolutely no similarities between that investigation and those particular portions of the novel concerning the same subject matter. However, any similarities are coincidental. It is also very important to note that all testimony, physical evidence, photographs, and every word spoken or uttered in the actual trial is public record. It can all be read and examined at the courthouse where the trial took place. There were also numerous newspaper articles at the time, documenting words uttered in testimony and detailing physical evidence presented.

It is hoped that anyone who reads this novel will get one very important message from it. If one has children, do your best to guide, counsel, and discipline them. What happened to the victim in this novel similarly happens to someone somewhere in the United States on almost a daily basis. This cruel and dangerous element of society does exist, and one must do everything possible to warn and protect their children of it. Once a young person begins associating with the wrong types of people, it is more often than not trouble from the get-go. Unfortunately in this story, the dangerous elements ended with a dramatic, fatal result.

Since the release of this novel, some events have changed in the life of the author. He has become a year and a half older, his health has declined significantly, and most importantly, the love of his life, his wife, Connie, passed away after a long illness. At this stage of the game, he does not want malice in his life, including upsetting people regarding *Murder in the Hoosier Corn*. Having said that, the fictional story the author made up is what it is, and the investigation that was used as an inspiration for this book was what it was. What is there left to say?

Made in the USA
Lexington, KY
13 May 2012